A Refugee's Rage

Also by Anthony Langford and published by Ginninderra Press

Bottomless River

Caged Without Walls

Pseudo Stars

Anthony Langford

A Refugee's Rage

A Refugee's Rage
ISBN 978 1 76041 774 1
Copyright © Anthony Langford 2019
anthonyjlangfordbooks.com
Cover: deviantart.com/m-tau

First published 2019 by
Ginninderra Press
PO Box 3461 Port Adelaide 5015
www.ginninderrapress.com.au

Contents

Caught Between Love and Loss

1

By the time she met him, he already had cancer. He refused to call it by its medical name, a not so rare but still less common form of lymphoma. It was, instead, the little slippery bastard that had been sent to test his will, just as he had begun building the house. She knew all about his dream project, but not his illness. That was due to his dogged character. His certainty that he could beat it on his own, would do, and that it would not interfere in his life. He also didn't want to scare her off, given that they'd only just begun dating. At twenty-seven, she was alluring, audacious and intelligent and with an appreciation for country life, a rare quality in a city-raised career girl. She seemed to share his exuberance for the mini homestead, the planned two-bedroom wooden cottage which was to be made from recycled and natural materials. There would be an extensive garden in the back to draw the eyes up to the mountain, as the town locals called it, though it was more a rocky outcrop atop a large, steep hill. It was covered with native trees and preserved by the council despite many capacious offers to acquire the land for private development.

Richard had been fortunate to purchase the land, as a deceased estate In mid 1994 for an equitable price. The existing building was way beyond repair. It needed demolishing and the land clearing. This he had done on his own, slowly over twelve months, as he simultaneously gathered the components required for the enterprise ahead. He discovered that some of the original beams could be put to good use, as well as two bedroom doors, a kitchen cupboard, a gramophone box, *sans* the gramophone, and the bath.

By the time he had met Rachel at a friend's Christmas function in '96, a party he had almost missed as it was on a Saturday night and would severely disrupt his two-hour weekend sojourns to the property, he was thirty-six, turning thirty-seven in February, and had already settled the foundations. Yes, he could have done a day's work and returned to the city for the function, but he knew that once he was in his haven, in the zone, he would not bother to leave. Much as it made him edgy, like a sock full of ants, he was soon delighted in his choice. He was immediately interested in her. Though they spoke cosily on several occasions during the night, Richard could tell that she was not as ebullient. By Sunday, he knew he was in trouble. Not only had he wasted a weekend, but he could not leave the memory of their time behind. He did not want a distraction.

Though well-built and reasonably popular with the opposite sex, particularly in his early twenties, the past eleven years (he remembered the exact moment; an epiphany in a bar) had been working towards building his own home in the country. Firstly, he had to raise his cash reserves in order to purchase the land. While most of his buddies were drinking away their incomes on weekends, he was doing a crash course in landscape gardening with a friend of his uncle's, knowing that the skills would one day be put to use, in addition to earning funds. He could ill afford a girl getting in the way now. Perhaps in a couple of years, ideally four, when the house would be complete. Apart from the initial concrete foundations, and eventually the electricity, he planned to do everything himself. He had even researched a block and tackle method of being able to raise the wall and roof beams on his own. Sure, he would need to call on family and friends occasionally but he wanted, needed, to know that when he finally lay in that bed, a second-hand metal four-poster that was already in the shed, though requiring the paint to be stripped and recoated, he would relish the knowledge that it was entirely of his making. His design. His work. His home.

The cancer was a natural shock, gilded with sick humour. His grandfather had died of the same thing when Richard was a boy, yet his father was still alive. He was too young to contemplate such a thing.

The intrusion was so severe, so inconvenient, that he refused to acknowledge it, to himself, to his family, to anyone. There was the house. And only the house. And then there was her.

He carried on working, though it was interrupted with the treatment that he required and the side effects of medication. There was even more pressure than before. He knew that he would not die, but his concern was that he would be too sick to work, hence almost missing the Christmas party he had agreed to sometime before. If he could ignore the sly bastard inside him, he could ignore a pretty face with a confident infectious laugh. But soon the image of her had taken space in his thoughts, and despite, mid-task, downing tools to disappear inside the shed to masturbate, he resumed work only to create little errors that he would never normally make. He conceded defeat and set about making Rachel his most urgent project.

2

Nothing worthwhile comes easy. She made him work for it. It wasn't until after several dates and numerous phone calls that she conceded to be a passenger on his motorbike to 'check out his turf'. He promised to take her back to the city if he was unable to convince her that they should accommodate themselves in the local tavern, yet she instantly fell in love with the view of the mountain and the trees and the quiet and the clean air and his obvious passion for his home. She shared his camp bed in the shed that night, making love for three hours and getting quietly drunk on local Cabernet Sauvignon.

In the following months, Rachel proved to be more than a worthwhile assistant. She possessed a sturdy constitution and was a quick learner. She even surprised herself, though she was unwilling to share this discovery with Richard. There were other contemplations she was also keeping private. It was all very new and arousing, and she admired her own verve for hard work, revelling in her new skills, yet there was something which did not sit quite right as far as their burgeoning relationship was concerned. Richard was a great guy, no doubt, physically strong with a will to match. A commitment to his dream which she could not help but respect to the point where she also felt committed. He had a deep affection for her without being overbearing, and everything appeared to be in place. So, what was lacking? She could not put her finger on it.

As 1997 wore on, some of the dazzle had faded and she began to make sense of her conflictions. She adored Richard's body and looked forward to sharing the double mattress that lay on straw matting in the shed and had replaced the camp bed. Their arduous lovemaking meant little sleep for the Sunday workload (he would not entertain a sleep-in) and the drive back to the city was extra tiresome. There was also a strong sense of camaraderie. But lust alone could not provide love. She did not share her confusing, non-specific feelings.

For the time being, she kept these deliberations to herself. She had invested too much to walk away. She had never worked harder in her life. It was imbued with a flavour of destiny. There was something special about the location. Was it the mountain that loomed over them? Or the moderate climate that ensured it was never too hot or too cold? Was it the birds that danced and sung every morning? Or the way the late afternoon light lit up the grass like white fire and made the tree leaves glimmer jade? She could not disentangle it, only that this place, this haven, had reached in and possessed her. The landscape was as much a part of her now as her future. And whether or not love was present didn't seem that important any more, as their bond was strong and there were other things beside love. Who knew? Perhaps it would arrive later, when the house was complete and they could concentrate more on each other. For now, as 1997 petered out, there was still so much more to do.

3

Before his thirty-eighth birthday in late January on a Thursday morning, not five minutes after sharing a joke, Richard collapsed at work. He was ferried to hospital by ambulance, unconscious. His boss called Richard's father. He immediately went to his son. Richard had regained consciousness but stressed that he did not want Rachel to know. His father promised but by Friday when he had not called her to arrange the weekend trip, Rachel called Richard's parents. They knew that they were betraying their son's confidence but felt it in his best interests if his girlfriend knew the full story. Aside from the fact that she had a right to know after a year of dating, Rachel could assist Richard more fully knowing the truth, not that it could be realistically hidden any longer.

At first, she was indignant, not that he was sick, or perhaps it was that, but that he had not told her. He had betrayed her in some way. He had forced her to live a lie. She decided not to see him or even call him that night. The next day, her passion had evened out somewhat and by Saturday, when they would normally be working, she drove to the hospital, riled that she should have to pay so much for the car park, as though the owners were capitalising on the misery of others.

Richard looked pale and gaunt and Rachel wondered why she hadn't noticed it before. She did not kiss him or say hello, instead wanting to know the reason behind his secrecy. He said, with an element of teenage cheek, that he was hoping it would all blow over soon, but that seemed dismissive to her. She stipulated that she deserved better than that and this was her life too and who did he think he was messing with it? He instantly knew he had made a mistake and fell serious. All of a sudden, he felt very vulnerable. He knew, for the first time, that he had underestimated Rachel. He realised that he could lose her and if that were to happen now, he would fall apart. When he began to cry, at last, the guilt surged in her, not that she should have made the effort to see him earlier, but that she comprehended that she did not love him the way he thought she did.

She went to him. Yet now, as if sensing her thoughts, he professed his love for her and without waiting for a response, asked her whether she felt the same.

She was taken aback by his raw emotions and the direct question. After an uncomfortable pause, she simply replied, 'Enough', though it wasn't the correct phrase for the question, or the answer he had hoped for. But he said no more and they embraced in silence.

4

Despite the doctor's warnings, with an array of pills to boost his reserves, Richard continued to work on the house, Rachel by his side. This was a time of urgency, not of scaling back. They did not talk of their relationship, instead focusing on their task, as though the work itself was a third person keeping them together, like a child perhaps, or as a cheaper metaphor, with the foundations established, the cement which kept them united.

Others now came forward with offers of help – Richard's parents, his work colleagues and even his younger brother Adam, who had never known physical work and only shared a cordial dynamic with his sibling. Reluctantly, Richard accepted it all, though he insisted on having a finger in every pie, the last say on every screw.

It was around this time, May '98, that Rachel met Dominic in the bottom-floor cafeteria, a place she rarely frequented, as she took her lunch to work most days, yet had gone to for a quick bite with her co-workers. He flirted with her unashamedly at the table parallel to her, as the seating area was tight to say the least. Soon, they were involved in conversation. Dominic worked for a small but prestigious accounting firm on the eighth floor. He was animated, keen for conversation and, from that first occasion, clearly her as well.

Rachel found him irritating and purely by coincidence, or perhaps it wasn't, found herself back at the cafeteria the next day. Though she acted impartial, she couldn't help but be drawn to his wit, his breadth of vocabulary and ability to turn a phrase, something she did not expect from a numbers man and the polar opposite to Richard's muted 'get on with it' manner. Aside from these early observations, she made the decision not to compare the two men, as one was entwined with her working life, in a matter of speaking, and the other, her personal life. Therefore, it was irrelevant. One didn't need to know about the other.

Her parents were also pushing her to consolidate her activities in the expected manner, as she was not getting any younger and that Richard, a gem of a man, would want to secure their union. She said she didn't feel any older than when she was twenty-one and, as neither of them wanted children, what did it matter? Besides, their immense building project was demonstrative of their loyalty. She was in for the long haul, no matter what. She knew that her parents really wanted her to get hitched for Richard's sake and his family's, as there was a chance that he might not be long for this world, but she wouldn't hear it said. She cut them off by reiterating that Richard was as determined 'as steel' to see his beloved venture through to the end. And that was that.

5

By August, it was clear that Richard would be unable to keep up the momentum, despite the positive news on his treatments. The cancer was loitering, perversely, but not progressing, yet the drugs were wearing him down. Vomiting while working was part of the routine. Yet he could not deny his diminished energy levels. He had already scaled back his Monday to Friday job, but it was not enough. By September's end, he was forced to give it up entirely. Work he could do without. However, he would not let the house go. Could not. His parents, other family members and friends, who had become a type of Team Richard, contributed funds to keep him going, and though he could only work for three to four hours a day, which had at one stage been fourteen, he could at least live in the shed and achieve a little something every day, albeit some days less than others.

Rachel showed up every weekend without fail. She also contributed financially when Richard allowed it. They never spoke of his illness. That's not the way Rachel worked, which unintentionally conformed to Richard's modus operandi. This non-verbal communicative manner had become the basis for their relationship.

Yet one night, in November, he surprised her by being candid while she was washing the dinner dishes and he was making lemon tea. He said that if he could not go on, she must stay and finish the house. Do it for them both. She was the only one who knew exactly how he wanted it. She was silent for a minute, watching the way the bubbles popped over her still hands, perhaps thinking she should be emotional, shed a tear or three. She at least owed his question a morsel of silence. She replied casually that of course she would, if it came to that, but it wouldn't because he had the will of a bear and he would beat his illness and that was the end of the discussion for now and into the future.

He was taken aback somewhat, as he had expected more from her, possibly a discussion of sorts, a little more emotion for a change, as he had been building up to this with no small amount of circumspection and now that it was out, was over too swiftly. Yet he accepted her response and finished off the tea, throwing the bags into the scrap bucket which would go onto the compost heap, doing his best to suppress the fear of his disease which had abruptly risen. It was mostly minimal, but it was always there, like sludge in the bottom of his stomach.

For some reason, he thought of the bad boy from school, Bruce, who was smaller than Richard but came from a dysfunctional family, and a ratty old wooden house that belonged to a bygone era and therefore wasn't quite of the same world. Bruce had promised to beat Richard up after school – for what reason, he had forgotten, but not the fear he was forced to endure for the rest of that extremely long day, at odds with the fight itself, which he could not avoid, and didn't really want to, rather than going through another day feeling sick and dismal. He received two fists to the face, which hurt, but then it was over and Bruce, having proved his point, left him standing holding his right swelling cheek and went back to that other dark world, which in retrospect, was probably a horrid place for a kid. The waiting was far worse than the outcome, yet there was no thought of his not surviving it.

This fight, however, was an unfair one, with much harsher odds. Who wants to wait? He didn't want that. And if things got worse, maybe he wouldn't.

6

The new morning brought fresh zeal, and the sludge bubbled away quietly out of view. When he was tired, it attempted to get the better of him and at times succeeded. Rest was important but it was merely treading water. It would not make the problem go away. The work had to come first. He had to focus. He had moved past his old stubborn pride of not seeking assistance and, with a concerted push from his team, the first room, the master bedroom, was completed by Christmas.

Richard's parents, plus his brother Adam and his partner, had checked into the local motel the night before, leaving the couple to spend Christmas Eve together, as was their wont. There was a hasty clean-up, a few decorations, and the entire family spent the big day in the one room. Adam had brought a cooler filled with beer and champagne, as the fridge in the shed was merely a bar fridge, something that Rachel periodically said was in need of an upgrade. Richard's mother went all out, bringing ham and turkey, freshly made rolls, mashed potato, gravy, green beans and a pumpkin pie. It was brought into fruition via the microwave in the shed as there was no oven let alone kitchen to speak of.

Rachel felt a little intimidated by this as she had only prepared a few cold hors d'oeuvres. She thought it was Richard's mother's way of showing her who was really capable of looking after her son as she flapped about like a mother goose dispensing orders. It was Rachel's turn to swallow her pride, for this day only, though she doubted that she could hide the disdain from her face. An adept poker face was not one of her strengths. This all took place in the master bedroom no less, as though spoiling the future, leaving a carpet of unpleasant memories, like a dog pissing to claim its territory. The two women had never really gotten along. It was a simmering current that had neither worsened nor lessened over time. Yet Richard seemed to be happy with the day's proceedings and that was enough.

His family wondered, without saying it, whether it would be their last Christmas with him. It was heavy on Rachel's mind too, mainly due to the obvious apprehensions coming from the others, which only served to make her more vexatious. Richard was the only one who did not ponder this hypothesis. The slippery bastard that lingered inside him would not get the better of him. It was merely a hindrance. At least, that's how he felt for the day, and maybe the champagne and beer had something to do with that. It was Christmas after all.

Richard's tenacity was reaffirmed early in the New Year when his doctor informed him that the cancer had gone into remission.

Richard took this as having beaten it. 'I told you I would kick that bastard's arse.'

He was told that it could return and that regular check-ups would still be necessary. He barely heard the advice. All he wanted was to notify Rachel so that they could get on with planning their lives together.

His family and friends were naturally elated and over the next few months, his colour and energy returned. The assistance he had been receiving on the house dried up. A shame perhaps, but to be expected. It didn't matter. Rachel was delighted and was glad to see his smile return, his genuine smile. It was as though they had gone back in time. Yet part of her felt empty, somehow heavy, as though she had taken on too much, even though real progress had been made with the house. Half of the doors were now in place, though without the extra manpower, the toil appeared to be without result, like a day in repetition.

She was still managing her job in the city during the week and was tired. Richard had not returned to work and, it seemed, wasn't intending to, living frugally on the property. He didn't take it well when Rachel said she would now be spending every second weekend at her flat to sleep. She couldn't keep the momentum up any more and it was selfish to expect her to. It meant that they would only see each other for four days and nights a month, but she was adamant. The house had evolved, yes, but she was burnt out.

Growing desperate to appease her, Richard suggested that she still come up every weekend but only work every second one, so that they could be together. She became immediately defensive, assuming that he was trying to control her, suffocate her, which he denied. Given the sacrifices he believed he had made in order to keep her happy, nothing seemed enough. Didn't she want to be with him? An argument flowered, bright, aromatic, bursting with piercing colour, carrying with it, like a flooded river, previous frustrations and suppressed emotions. The dispute reached a point where he believed she had no recourse, which was the point she went to the door, marched to her car and drove to the city.

7

Dominic suggested that she leave Richard. Just a suggestion, mind you. As she was quick to point out, Dominic was heavily biased. He replied by saying that he could not wait forever and all their sneaking about was frustrating him no end. Richard appeared to be better too and her guilt had lessened. Therefore, wouldn't it be more prudent to cut their losses? She restated, as her one and only line of defence, that she had invested too much time, effort and emotion in the whole damned thing. Besides, part of her was now at the base of that mountain. He asked her if she had become a tree. She called him a prick. She also said that if he couldn't wait around to see what the outcome would be, then maybe he should be the one to cut his losses. This exchange also escalated into a dust-up and, after spending a lonely but necessary fortnight alone, Rachel returned to the country.

8

Richard's thirty-ninth birthday was a quiet affair, at his insistence, as he planned to have a huge fortieth in his new house. Any family member who attempted to suggest the prospect of a bleaker reality was quickly though politely dismissed. Rachel had brought with her a small carrot cake with icing, his favourite, one candle and a bottle of Californian Cab Sav. That night they rejoiced quietly in the shed. It felt like the old days. They made love, though not to their earlier excesses, but both felt fulfilled. It seemed as though they had reclaimed their step. Rachel was soothed. She hoped it would last.

9

Spring came early. It was the warmth which brought the snake out of the shade, and towards the long shallow pit where Richard was kneeling in, securing the water pipe. The snake was to his left but far enough around to be out of his field of vision.

Rachel, with two plastic cups of tea, saw it meandering across the dirt. She was no expert and didn't know if it was a rattlesnake or a gopher but it was clearly a full adult. She had seen a couple scuttling off into the brush in her time at the property but never one so brazen. Perhaps it hadn't noticed Richard but it was tracking towards his exposed legs, as he always wore shorts when working, even in winter. She knew she had to warn him and that all she had to do was call out his name, but she seemed unable to do it. It was ridiculous. It wasn't as though she was frozen in fear, though she was fearful of the thing, but rather that this presented an opportunity which she had not foreseen and could possibly solve the burden her life had become, and wasn't it a disgusting thought, a horribly self-interested one, but at the same time, an attractive solution almost too good to pass up. She really didn't have to do anything. Rather, do nothing.

The snake oozed over the lip of the trough. Rachel was literally stiff now like a mummified exhibit, a mere spectator in her unravelling destiny. Richard promptly scrambled to his feet and ran backwards and shouted 'Fuck me', having sensed it. Rachel called out his name as though his actions had loosened her tongue. She knew she would say that she didn't see it until the split second before he did and hope he didn't recall the moments before when her footsteps approached from the shed. She was sure he wouldn't, as he had a tendency to zone out when working on his own, unlike when working with her or others, as he had to keep an eye on the efficiency of their labour.

For its part, the snake was equally as startled and flipped almost a hundred and eighty degrees and shot off into the copse from where it had come.

<h1 style="text-align:center">10</h1>

In the second weekend of May, while Rachel was 'out country', Dominic took it upon himself to visit the little town that he had heard so much about but had never seen. He wasn't about to allow himself to be kept at length forever. He needed to know more about Rachel's other life if he was to win her completely. Though forty-two, a father of an eleven-year-old boy and still married, he had been separated for over two years and shared a house with a young primary teacher named Curtin, who was quite conservative and had no idea that Rachel, who stayed over on occasion, was in another relationship.

Dominic checked in to a room upstairs at the local tavern, one of two in town, called Stanley's Brew 'n' Bar. After two beers sitting out front on a wooden bench, he garnered a taste for it and decided that it was unlikely that the couple would come into town as it was now after four-fifteen and, even if they did, Richard wouldn't recognise Dominic, not being aware of his existence.

Dominic wasn't to know that while at the bar ordering his second beer, the couple had driven past in her car on their way to the one and only supermarket just a little further down the road. They were on their way back when Dominic emerged from the front bar, having purchased his third beer, and was taking in the rather subdued local atmosphere, by comparison, of this quaint but nowhere town that Rachel had adopted, when he saw her car tracking steadily past.

Perhaps knowing that she was being watched, as people often do, Rachel turned to investigate. She didn't have time to do a double take, nor did her mouth fall open, but there was enough of a discrepancy in her expression for Richard to observe. He enquired as to what she had seen that made her stare so. She could not deny that she had and said, after being unable to think of anything else, that she thought she had recognised someone. She immediately regretted it, but a delay would have been more suspicious. When pushed, she had to say yes, it had been a man, but that she was wrong and maybe she was simply tired and no she did not need to go back and check but that he should stop being so neurotic.

She could barely contain her fury at Dominic's intrusion into her private domain. She suffered long and hard throughout the next twenty-six hours, trying to keep up a normal pretence for Richard's sake but unsure that she was successful. By the time she arrived at her darkened unit back in the city, the animosity had ebbed a little and, even though she had rehearsed what she planned to say ten times over, she opted not to call Dominic after all. Not tonight. Not ever. She would not allow any man to put her in such a delicate and uncompromising position again, unless she had put herself there first, which she might already have done by being in a form of dependent guilt-oriented relationship with Richard, but that was beside the point.

She went to work the next day expecting communication from Dominic. When she received it, she ignored it and managed to deflect his every call and the ones from that day forth. She knew there had been a turning of the page and even though there were many residual feelings, it was time to do the right thing and let Dominic go.

11

In July, cuddled in the dark, she dropped the L word for the first time. She knew it had been developing, strengthening, but it sounded awkward coming out of her mouth. She wondered if he had noticed.

Richard sat upright and turned on the lamp. 'You said it, finally.'

'What?' she said, unable to prevent a smirk. 'You know I hate all that romance crap.'

'You said it,' he beamed, ruffling her hair like a child.

She smiled coyly. 'Don't expect to hear it again.'

'I knew it. You've just been in denial. Come on, let's stop playing games and get married.'

She blinked, aware of the shadows on the tin wall behind him, a looming Richard, an exaggerated caricature, a horror movie clown with a perverse sense of humour.

'We'll get stuck into the work. I'll bring the family back in. Finish it enough by January so we can have my fortieth. We'll have a house-warming, birthday party and engagement party, all in one.' He sat taller, as though the idea had only just struck him. 'Six months and we can be living in the house. Together. Pretty fantastic idea, don't you think?'

It was too much, too fast, his face too eager, like a boy, forcing her to look away. 'Jesus, you'll be trying to knock me up next.'

'Well, you know…'

'I'm not that sort of woman. I told you that from the beginning.'

'Okay. We can talk about that later. Don't…' He took hold of her arm and cupped her face. 'Let's just get married. It doesn't have to be all boring and traditional. Mum will get over it. We'll do it right here in the backyard. Nice and quick. Simple. And then we'll party all night.'

She tried to smile but it was a partial grimace. She had opened the valve but now she was drowning. 'Richard…' but she didn't know what else to say.

'Don't answer now. Just think, a low-key affair with a big booze-up. Maybe a pig on the spit.'

She remained silent but she already knew her answer. She couldn't tell him now. His excitement level was enough to destroy him. There would be an expenditure of emotion and a staccato sleep would follow. Above all else, she was tired.

12

They didn't discuss his off-the-cuff marriage proposal, which she feared was far from spontaneous. He believed that she was thinking it over and didn't want to force the issue by raising the subject, instead waiting for her to do so. Rachel secretly hoped he wouldn't bring it up again.

Thirty-four days later, after a protracted dizzy spell, Richard, urged on by his mother, was accompanied back to his doctor. Playing it safe, they managed to book in a series of scans the following day. Rachel was unaware, as he didn't want her to worry unnecessarily. His mother thought she should worry as that was part of her role as a partner, as a woman, but Richard thought his mother was being more disagreeable than usual.

On the Friday afternoon, Rachel received a call at work. She was a little put out to hear Richard's voice, as it was due to be her weekend off and her non-working days in the city alone and with her friends were highly valued. When he explained that he wanted to talk to her, she knew from his tone that it was not good. In fact, it could only mean one thing. She mentioned this fact. He said he wanted to talk to her in person, but she insisted that he tell her immediately, which he reluctantly agreed to. The cancer was back, and this time he did not refer to it as the little bastard, which informed her of its seriousness. The tumour was not in its usual position, which explained why it had been missed during the check-ups, giving it a chance to grow undetected.

She demanded the ultimate prognosis, which he was still avoiding. 'Yes! Over the fucking phone!'

He caved. Though the doctor talked in a roundabout fashion, the crux of it remained that, more than likely, he would be dead before Christmas. She hung up.

She went home, stony-faced, keeping it together until after the second white wine, when she began to unravel. She called Dominic. He was there within the hour, with two bottles of wine, though she had only asked for one. As he poured, she wanted him to convince her that she was not evil, had not been an unfaithful bitch, though it was impossible to dismiss her infidelity. He passed her the wine, saying that she could be a bitch at times but she was definitely not evil. She continued, voice level as though he had not spoken, saying that she was a cold, heartless cunt for not shedding a tear since the afternoon's call and that she was going straight to hell. She didn't go to church aside from at Easter and Christmas but she did believe in something, which meant that she was a partial agnostic or some such label, but Rachel had never been one for labels and went out of her way to avoid having any of them attached. She wanted to be unique and felt as though she was, and yet, it seemed to have come at a price.

Dominic, sitting by her on the couch with a glass also, said that it was testament to her good character that she felt such guilt, especially when she was with a man she didn't love. This put her on guard once again. She swore that she did love Richard and that she'd been fighting it; for what reason, however, she could not answer. Dominic said that she'd been fighting the notion because in actuality she was in love with Dominic. He then went to embrace her but she pulled away and told him to back up and that he was only there to support her and provided he didn't try a juvenile consoling tactic, spend the night as a friend as she was feeling vulnerable to the point where she didn't trust herself. Dominic asked if she was talking about self-harm and hoped that she wasn't, as that was ridiculous, she wasn't the type. It was only for weak individuals, which she certainly was not.

Rachel proceeded to get very drunk. She walked around her unit, ranting, sporadically shuffling through her music for a particular song and it was soon late and she was singing to a particular album by a particular band and perhaps it was deliberate or perhaps it was some unseen force working its way through her as the song was entitled 'Better Man'.

When she woke, she was disoriented. She didn't recall going to bed. Dominic was next to her. Was he naked? She peeked under the sheet. He had underwear on but that was all. It didn't confirm nor usurp her concerns. She couldn't recall if Dominic had made a move on her or not. She felt herself, though that wasn't a confirmation either, yet for the time being concluded that there had been no sex. She watched Dominic sleep for approximately fifteen minutes while speculating her future. She played through various scenarios but came to no real conclusions. With an urge to be vagarious, she reached down and took a hold of his penis and brought it to life.

As Dominic was leaving, roughly an hour and a half later, he tried to kiss her again but she held him back and said the sex had been nothing more than a goodbye moment. She was aware of how cold she came across but efficiency was paramount. She was thankful for the comfort he had provided but they would not be seeing each other again. She closed the door and went straight to the window to let in fresh air.

13

From that weekend onwards, Rachel did not leave Richard's side. He was on heavy medication to slow the effects of the cancer and lessen his pain. It had spread throughout his spine and was, therefore, inoperable. He was very lethargic, requiring two naps a day, like 'a fucking baby', as he put it. Though he was now permanently stationed at his parents', Richard insisted that Rachel live in the house too. His parents had no choice but to allow it, even though it caused friction with his mother, something his father couldn't quite understand, especially given the circumstances. The house had become a hot bed of tension, mostly away from Richard's presence, though he was not ignorant, merely too tired to care about any cattiness.

One bright afternoon in October when it was evident what the outcome would be, though still not to be discussed, Rachel lay on top of the bed next to her sleeping, underweight partner. She speculated as to what might have been, living in the gorgeous house that they had created, away from the poisonous city that she was sure was responsible for her initial lack of depth and self-centred attitude. Why did this have to happen to her? Almost within reach of achieving her dream. Their dream. All of that hard work. Especially for Richard, who had put his life on hold to forge a better tomorrow, only to have his destiny betray him. She felt empty once more. Deceived. She had finally made the right decision by getting rid of Dominic, without the benefit of time to prove her loyalty to Richard.

Overcome by her emotions, she tried to wake him, but couldn't. His face was thin, aged, but with an element of the child within, as he once was, the photos she had seen, a lifetime ago and only yesterday.

Instead, she lay patiently by his side and waited almost two hours until he woke naturally. Having slept an hour longer than usual, it was approaching six p.m.

She smiled with affection, head still on the pillow. 'I want to do it,' she whispered. 'I will. I'll marry you.'

He stared at her, demeanour unchanged, but by no means emotionless. He did not respond.

'I'm saying yes, you silly boy. Let's get married. Right here in the backyard. Or at the house if you want. Like you wanted to. Did you want to do it there?'

'Rachel…'

'It will be beautiful, my sweet. And I want you to talk to your doctor about the possibility of us having a baby. And if you're not up to it, maybe we can get the sperm extracted. We'll do IVF if we have to.'

He gave the slightest of shakes.

She went on, becoming more despondent when he had not responded the way she had thought he would. 'And if it's a boy, maybe we could name him after you. Is that okay or is it too corny? Maybe it will be a girl. A girl would be nice too. What would you call her? What would you call him? We've never talked names. Or babies. But…'

'We're not getting married.'

'What do you mean? Why?'

'That's not who you are, Rachel. It never was. You made me learn that, the hard way.'

She erupted in tears, almost like a coughing fit, severe enough to cause her pain in her sternum but she was unable to stop it.

'I'm doing you a favour,' he said composedly, hoping she could hear him above her heavy wet coughs, as he did not want to repeat himself. 'In a year from now, six months, you'll be glad of it. I'm setting you free. It's the way you would have ended up eventually.'

She wanted to defend her emotions, her earlier choices and now her current decision. Her previous state of mind had only been a denial. The long way round. Couldn't he see that? This was how she felt now. It was more real than anything she had ever known. Yet her throat was heaving and her head felt like tearing open and she couldn't articulate it.

He laid a hand on her forearm, but it had no effect.

14

In early November, she drove Richard back to the country to see the house. He sat on the sand by the back door, where the porch should have been by now but had not even reached its earliest stages. He remained there for over an hour, looking up at their mountain. She promised him that she would finish the house, just as he wanted. He was pleased but they did not wallow in the finality of their situation and moved on to discussing where to place their lead-light windows. They talked about the kitchen and how it should be equipped and continued their journey through the other rooms, positioning imaginary furniture, even though they had discussed it previously, as though to cast the final decisions.

As they were leaving, he said he would return and that he was not done with yet and there was the New Year to look forward to, being a new century, no matter what the doomsayers said about the world's technology imploding or some such rubbish and it was just another scare tactic. Rachel agreed serenely, neither with confidence nor pessimism.

One night in December as Richard watched his two beloved ladies decorate the Christmas tree, he calmly and quietly told them that he would be leaving the country house to Rachel. His mother was astounded. Rachel kept decorating. A curt restrained discussion ensued as his mother conjectured if it wasn't best kept in the family, as a memorial. Richard said his mind was made up. Besides, he had already filed his will with the lawyer. Rachel softened the mood to some degree by saying that any family member was welcome to stay wherever they wished, especially Richard's parents.

Every night, wondering if it were to be his last, Rachel smothered his face in kisses and told him how much she loved him and how he was her soulmate and always would be and how sorry she was that she had taken so long to realise it. Sometimes he said nothing. On other occasions he would say that it was not the house that was the pinnacle of his life but Rachel, and how lucky he had been to find her.

Christmas was a magnificent affair. All of the family was present, knowing how fortunate they were to still have Richard around, even if all the commotion made him very tired.

He slept a lot in the ensuing days. People dropped by to see him. There were impromptu gatherings around his bed, mainly reflective affairs, often jovial. Whether he was aware of it or not was hard to judge, and perhaps it didn't matter.

He hung around to see in the new millennium, telling everyone that while he was glad that he had made it to see the new century, he preferred the old one. It was a comment that grew more entertaining over time and would be repeated by Adam many times, suggesting the bond he had with his brother was stronger than it actually had been.

Rachel was debating with herself as to the final words she would say to him, knowing that it was important and would always stay with her. Yet it was difficult to tell when Richard was lucid. He could have his eyes open and not be aware of her, or with eyes closed, perfectly alert. There was no one size fits all scenario for his state of being. It was minute by minute. Second by second.

These prophetic words, which she had yet to decide upon, became immaterial. Richard entered into a coma sometime during the early hours of January the third. He spent less than twenty-four hours in hospital before he died, officially passing at twelve-fourteen in the morning, without ever waking up, unfortunately not fulfilling his final wish, which was to kick the big bucket at home, though keeping with his belief that unless hospitals could be made more fun, he would never be spending much time in one.

That same morning, Rachel returned to her flat. Any dealings with the family, especially the cranky old hawk, during the next week, were sparse. At the funeral she nodded and hugged and patted and lowered her head during the right places, hoping to hide her lack of tears. She had cried in her own space and in her own time and didn't need to perform on cue in a public place and was sceptical of those who did.

After the funeral, Rachel set about getting to work. She wanted the house finished and did not want to spend another year doing it. She decided, had already decided, to take out a loan, and hired two men to complete the work. She had no interest in doing any of it herself. She had completed more than her quota and without Richard to guide her, didn't feel confident enough anyway. She wanted it done with. She would fulfil her promises to Richard, but never said that she would do it all on her own.

15

The family organised a barbecue for what would have been Richard's fortieth birthday. Rachel suspected it would be more like the funeral version two and decided not to go. More eulogising and blame-seeking was the last thing in the world she could endure. She knew her absence would damage an already fragile relationship but justified it by telling herself that she was single-minded in her endeavours to complete Richard's dream. And there weren't many family members she liked spending time with anyway, except Richard's father, who was the only one who came close to resembling his son, unlike the rest, who were imbued with the genes of his mother. Lamentably, Richard's father was under considerable pressure to appease his wife and wasn't allowed enough capacity to truly be her friend. Such are the cruel, often comedic ironies of life.

Progress was swift. The windows went in, some with lead-lighting as discussed with Richard, like the front and rear doors that somehow were a part of him. She knew if she thought about it for too long, it could make her sentimental, so she did not wallow. Soon the electrics were in and the kitchen was finished, after a false start when the wrong type of glue was used on the tiles. The final extensive task was the inclusion of the porch, which seemed fitting somehow. He had sat there in its place during his final visit.

There was still a lot of other work to be done, such as the garden and the furnishings, both of which she had verbally sketched out so that Richard could approve (he had closed his eyes to visualise it and had drifted off). They had also agreed upon the type of vegetation so that, in years to come, the rear mountain view would never be obscured.

Rachel held on to her apartment in the city for the time being and spent the first real night in the house on a Friday, 31 March. She felt a great deal of satisfaction in her toils, a corporate city girl, as she sat on her couch that she had picked up locally for a good price. Like many of the fixtures, it was more reasonably priced than it would have been in the city and of a more natural, homemade quality. She listened to the crickets and the birds as the fading, trickling light removed the mountain top from view.

Yet by the next day, she felt terribly alone. She was used to a solitary lifestyle in the city but this was different. There had always been someone around. It didn't feel right. Amidst nature it felt unnatural. And once again, the desolate feeling returned, a void that needed illumination – not love, nor the need for a man, as she could live without both, but companionship. The house was designed for it.

The following weekend, Dominic joined her. To hear from her had not surprised him, but the invitation did. Now he was the one making the weekend journeys. At last, Rachel knew that this was how it should be. She wasn't sure she loved Dominic, not yet, but she did feel relaxed around him and had no qualms telling him her every thought, no matter how dark and borderline obsessive, without worrying about offending him. She even told him to fuck off, which she had made the mistake of doing once with Richard, who was quiet and stoic and sensitive. Dominic understood her. She wasn't sure that Richard ever did.

Towns are not small but empty and it takes a strong community, if not a little weighty on gossip, to fill them. The word was out and within several weeks, Richard's parents contested the will. Rachel knew exactly who was driving it. She also knew which people to cut off in town – only a few, those who had been close to Richard, as any one of them could have been responsible for the 'fucking pathetic 007-style spying'.

In the months to come, she would cease having much to do with the town residents at all, preferring to shop, and now work, in a much larger town some thirty kilometres away. It was clear that the pair of them were setting up a future together and in a surprisingly short amount of time, Dominic relocated his work, albeit with a substantial reduction in earnings.

The will was very clear. There was nothing to dispute and after concise proceedings, Rachel came out on top and had her legal fees covered. Victory was gratifying, if not exquisite, as she had raised ample animosity towards her once prospective mother-in-law, especially during the stressful and money wasting wrangle, which she felt was more based on revenge than property.

Finally, Rachel felt complete. She had come out the other side, battle-weary, yes, but ready for the next, hopefully more moderate stage of her life, with a man whom she may or may not have needed but loved enough.

16

It had been a significant adjustment for both. By the beginning of 2001, Dominic had become increasingly cantankerous, more on the aggressive side. She assumed he had been having difficulty adjusting to a way of life that had been of her making and not his. He had said as much. Yet it struck her that while busy in the garden, a chore that wasn't, he had been worse lately, not better. They'd had more arguments in the past few weeks than ever before.

That night, after he chastised her for pausing the video *Memento*, during what he deemed a crucial scene, she yelled, 'I have to do a fucking piss, Dominic. Is that all right with you?'

He sighed heavily. 'Jesus Christ, couldn't you have waited a couple of minutes?'

Standing over him she said, 'Fine. Press play and I'll piss right here.'

He shook his head, looking at the frozen though wobbly image of a confused Guy Pearce. 'Do whatever the fuck you want.'

She studied him, frowning, hands on hips. He said nothing. It appeared she had to push further. She was tired of pussyfooting about. She seemed to have less patience for games as she grew older. 'What is your problem lately?'

'Don't worry about it. You wouldn't understand.'

'I'm a pretty smart girl. I think I just might.'

'Well, you should. If you could just turn that big searchlight brain of yours away from yourself for five minutes, you might notice.'

'What the hell are you going on about? Notice what exactly?'

'Ah, forget it. I'm wasting my time. You don't observe anything. You're too inward.'

He continued staring at the television, as though it was still playing, so she manoeuvred herself back and forth in front of him. 'Dominic, don't play the cryptic with me. Just spit it out.'

He looked up at her, lastingly before responding. 'Fine. You'll think I'm mad but I don't really care.'

'Go on.'

'I lie in bed at night, and all I can think is that it's his bed.'

'What?'

'I go to the bathroom in the middle of the night and I'm looking around at the shadows, half expecting to see him.'

She scoffed, with a smile that wasn't convincing. 'Don't be ridiculous.'

'Do you know I actually look at the couch on the way to the toilet, just in case he's sitting there? I swear to God, I can feel him here.'

She began to move off, towards the bathroom; it crossed her mind that this very movement was the subject of the conversation she was now turning her back upon.

Dominic stood and went after her. 'Don't walk away from me! I'm trying to talk to you. You asked and I'm telling!'

She swivelled. 'All right, but I think you're being a cranky prick just for the hell of it.'

'Rachel, can't you feel it? He's everywhere.'

His tone had changed enough for her to lower her guard a little. This wasn't just a tantrum, as he was prone to on occasion. There was something serious in his demeanour. As though he were genuinely troubled.

'I mean it. He's here. In the kitchen, looking through the windows.'

'Are you talking about ghosts, Dominic? I didn't think accountants believed in ghosts.'

'Don't fucking patronise me, Rachel. He's in the walls. In the fucking walls!'

'I finished this house off,' she uttered, but it was without conviction. She realised her hand was resting clumsily on her head.

'You know what I'm talking about.'

She shook her head, almost whispering now, 'You're insane.'

Now that she thought about it, and had done before, she'd experienced the sensation that Richard really was lingering around the next corner, the next room, but especially near the shed. It unnerved her to go near it. She had never spoken of it, had barely acknowledged it to herself other than an uncomfortable feeling. But now that the subject had been activated, she admitted to herself that she was terrified of the shed. It was like a flame to a long fuel-soaked sheet.

Yet they were both stubborn, particularly during an argument, and it continued for another minute or two before she broke it off to pee. He hit stop on the video, worried the spinning head drum would damage the tape and when she returned, they resumed the altercation, not unlike the remote between them. From pause to play, but at a more subdued pace.

Another ten minutes passed until they both conceded that there was some residual effect, a presence, an afterthought, a feeling, paranoia, guilt, regret, but a certain indefinable something that prevented them both, especially Dominic, from being able to relax and call the place they lived home.

'It is a home,' he said, 'but it doesn't belong to us.'

17

The breeze wafted from the sky to the golden grasses at the base of the mountain. Trees robust and protective. Branches meditating. Leaves flowing in the wind like a green wave lapping the shore. A more serene atmosphere you could not wish for, yet the couple screamed at each other frequently over the weeks ahead, all the while refusing to capitulate to a spirit or the idea of haunting or any such bullshit. Articulating those very notions reduced them to something less than they felt they were. Inwardly, both felt that Richard was present in some form, that he was in fact orchestrating the tension in a bid to separate them and was amused at the chaos he had instigated. Other than what they had admitted on the night of the original squabble, his name was not uttered, as they were both practical people after all and didn't believe in such things. They skirted around the subject while not acknowledging its core. In all truth, neither could deny Richard's sweat in every wall and physicality upon every rivet and, perhaps most of all, the lingering injustice of his premature death.

It was ultimately brought to a head after yet another disturbed sleep, when Dominic shuffled zombie-like off to work. He phoned from his office less than two hours later and told Rachel in a monotone, unapologetic voice that, with or without her, he was moving to be closer to his work, where he had already developed a steady clientele.

Once upon a time, she would have hung up on him, or screamed down the line, but she accepted it quietly. She fell silent for a time, wondering if she could or would stay on in the house on her own. She then understood that she did need Dominic after all, which disappointed her, as she thought she had never needed anyone, much less a man, but then, she had rarely been without one. Perhaps she had been mistaken all these years as to her true personality. Completely. She was instantly depressed, defeated, with a sense of a real physical weight to her body. She had wasted years on the house, which had once been a dream but had become a sort of a torment. A cheeky uncompromising vine twisted around her happiness, preventing it from breathing, similar, in a perverse way, to the deceitful cancer which had taken Richard.

After hanging up the phone, she walked slowly out the back door and stood looking past the garden, which was doing charmingly well. In a few years, it would really come into its own. She knew that when it did, she would not be living there. She gazed with a kind of numb respect to the mountain, and knew that somehow, Richard was there looking down at her, perhaps with a smile, saying, that this is how it was meant to be.

'Okay,' she said. 'You can have your way. I know this is what you want. You win. I know I'm not the person you thought I was. I don't even know who I am sometimes. Maybe I don't know me at all. I feel like I'm caught between two worlds. Like there's two of me. But I am trying, Richard. I want to try. I'm going to. And I'll leave this to you. It was always yours. You have it back. But please know that I'm sorry.'

Much as it deflated her pride to admit defeat, it had not been a total loss. She was out of the city, a place and a lifestyle that was over rated and overpriced. She was in a relationship and there was still the potential to build on that. She might or might not love him. She was still undecided. It seemed she could never be certain of love. Perhaps she did not trust it. Feasibly, the entire proceedings from meeting Richard to now was a natural progression of broken plans, misfortunes, let-downs and surprises that constitutes the chaotic order/disorder of life.

It didn't have to be a catastrophe. She could rent the house out. Being only two hours from the city and an area affluent in tourism, she could turn it into a self-contained cottage, rather than a bed and breakfast, so she would not have to spend one more night under the roof she helped erect, and under the spell of Richard's ever-present gaze.

On Friday 23 June, Rachel left the house, in a way returning it to the palm of the mountain.

A Refugee's Rage

Two Halves of Nothing

'Bad time. Maybe the stars not watch us this day.'

I

It is a hot day. Not yet, but soon. It is my day, Alexandru Day. Every day is Alexandru Day. Alexandru is good Romanian name. It says 'Defender of Mankind'. It is my name.

I sit on the steps. In the park, where I sleep. By the concrete square. Where the break-dancers come with their cardboard to make the dance. To get the money and stay all day. At night they become drunk. It is too early. The square is unfilled. Some of them live in little apartment with family. Others live here. In the park. Many of my friends are asleep. They like the night hours best. Most of young homeless are immigrants. Like me. Many peoples hate us. We know this and don't worry. We are strong. Together.

I light a cigarette. The wind is dead. The smoke stays with me like a friend. Some old people walk in the park. They look bored. The metro station is not far. Vittorio Emmanuele. Some go there now. I know some faces but most pretend to not see me.

Look at this couple. I see them every day. The man, he never look at me. But the woman, she look. I don't know what she think. Maybe she want my young body because her man now has peaches like her. I mean like the tits. Maybe I look like her grandson. Maybe she wonder what a dirty Romanian, here in the country of Italiano.

I flick my cigarette like a catapult. It fall in the grass. Sometimes at night, if I am bored and tired of the world, I can hit the cats. It is a good game. There are too many cats in Roma. Many live over the fence of the Giardini Piazza Vittorio. Because not many people like them. They fight at night. Not even cats like them. Sometimes stop me to sleep. This make me mad. And my friends too. So the next day, we play the Game. One time, a stranger I did not know, played the Game. He put orange cat on fire. It run very fast. It soon a more orange cat. We laugh very hard for many hours. Still, I like to think of it.

I walk to the gate that face the Via Conte Verde. In the wall is a little fountain with the water from the spring. It is good water to drink. There are lots of them. I like this one. I have a good drink. I wash on my *fesso* and my hair. My hair is short now. Some days back, my friend cut it for three cigarettes. She use a special shape glass from bottle. She is *bella*. Not her. Her cuts with the hair. Her *fesso* is like cat's bum hole, all screwed up in middle.

I walk back to the park. Off the path. Under two rows of trees that are long. I do this every day to kill the sleep. Before I wake my friend, Gogu. He is good friend. He is same age plus one year. But not smart like me. Not as handsome *fesso* like me. I have one cigarette left now. I always must have two in the morning. If I have many, I give one to Gogu when he wake up. But now I only have this one. So I smoke it now.

I walk around. This is the best part of the day. I don't wish to kill it by my thinking. If I think too long about *La Vita* then I get sad. I do not think my life will get better. Because I am Romanian. I can speak good Italiano as I have been here for half my life. Which is eight years. But I will always be immigrant to them. It could be more bad. I could look like Gogu. He is with the one eye that looks to the south, no matter which part of the world he is looking. I say to him, 'Gogu! What is on ground?' or 'Have you hit your toe, Gogu?'

Sometimes, when there is big group of people I say, 'Gogu must have a stiff one, because he is looking at it!' Gogu always chase me on this last one. He get really mad and beat me with his fists. My hair is short now, so he can pull on it no longer. I still laugh but sometime I have to drop him with my fist, when he take it for too long.

I walk behind the big rock by the bush. Where we sleep. We both have blanket. I have plastic bag for bed. Gogu has the cardboard. Cardboard is no good in winter or if there is *molto acqua*. He still asleep. His feet is on the grass. I will make a joke. I pull out my little man. I almost laugh and give it away. I push and the piss is come. I wet it all over Gogu's feet. I laugh. He pull his foot in fast and sit up. I piss a little on his cardboard.

'Hey! You *cafone!*'

'Don't call me arsehole! I piss on your *fesso!*' But I laugh too much and stop pissing now.

Gogu jump up and wipe his feet on the grass. 'Oh you! You!'

I'm laughing too hard.

'*Vaffanculo!*'

He has told me to fuck myself. Nobody tell Alexandru this. I kick out and smack his head and he fall. But not hard as I could.

'Eh…' He rubbing his head.

'Get up now,' I say. 'Let us go get the food.'

'Not do that again. I was dreaming about a girl. So pretty.'

'The only girl you will have ever is a girl cat. Let's go.'

'*Si. Si.*'

2

There are many places to get a little food, but never much. We are walking through the Piazza Dante. We get our morning food here at fruit stall. But only every five or six days. It is easy to get the food. I am smart. We do not come to same place every day. Even now, I think we find a new fruit stall.

The sun is climbing. There is many peoples about. Going to do many things. Always with the hurry. We walk the Via Merulana. The tourists are here. Already early. Every day a new collection. Every day, new ears for our old story.

We walk into another street and pass the road. Our place, the Pastry House. Most have their pastries behind the glass but not this one. It is kept by a husband and wife who are old. There are people there, standing for the coffee. Gogu is talking but I am not listening. I am waiting for the moment. It will not be long. It is always at this time. Ten minutes go past. Fifteen. Then the shop is quieter. The man takes his leave. He enjoy the morning shit. I shit when I feel like it, but only three days afar. Sometimes, a week or more.

'Shut up. The time is right.'

I run, pass over the road. The motorbikes and cars try to hit me and beep but I am too fast. Gogu is too slow. I am looking at which pastry I want. I move to put the woman worker behind a café drinker, so she not see me. Gogu is behind me. I step forward slow. Like a cat after a insect. I pick two from the stack. I turn to look at Gogu so he can take my place. It take me a second to work out as his one stupid eye is looking down. But it is the other which is wide, which is the most worry. I turn back. The husband has walk back. Maybe his shit not working. He see me and I am uncovered. He yell out. We are broken. I reach and lift a stack of pastry in my arms. Stupid Gogu is still standing.

'Run, *stupido*!' I leave the shop fast. We are running into the sun. The husband yell out behind. I am not worry with him but other Italianos who would like to beat on two young Romanian.

I drop a pastry and then another. Accident. Gogu went to pick them up but I yell him not to be a *stronzo* and keep to the running. I run to a smaller street and drop another pastry. Gogu is slower. Now I hear motorbike after us which is not the *carabinieri* but man who I thought would happen. Italiano want to be the hero man. I quickly look to see what I must do. I was not in this mood for today but now I must be. There is only one motorbike. I look for a street where it is small and the cars parked tight. I run there. He will have to be slow and now he slow. Now I have the strong chance. I drop the pastries, he think I not let them go. I wait for him for two seconds and jump and push him off motorbike and it fall on his leg. I take the up hand further and jump up and I land on his shoulder and *fesso*. My shoes are soft and not so good with holes but I can push down fast and not hurt my foot. I keep pushing down very hard so he is not getting up. I see Gogu back between cars where he pull over to let motorbike chase me.

'Your help is not so good, Gogu!'

He come out with his hands up and the sorry in the Romanian way. I stick to Italian curses like *cafone*. I tell him to go pick up my pastries because he has none. If he lucky, I maybe give him one. He does it. There is seven, maybe.

We leave now, quickly. The hero Italiano no hero no more. We go to other streets. Now no more with the chase.

'I got the hero man, Gogu. You see?'

'Yes, Alexandru. But now we cannot go to café no more.'

'I know this, *stronzo*.'

I no wish for anyone to see us near Our Park with the pastries. I will have to eat them all, but this is okay. I no have to worry for food tonight. I tell Gogu if I give him pastry extra, he can give me cigarettes. Usual days, we have to beg. And follow tourists with the old story so they give us money. I get tired of this. If I can rest for a day, I will do this.

We have taken an hour or more to where we are now. The Piazza Croce Rossa. We sit. The sun is very hot now. We in much relief. We have food for our stomachs. I keep two pastries. I can hide in my street to take back to the park. I tell Gogu he can get other. When he get the cigarette. He thinks I mean to beg and go with the old story. But I say no. Not today. I explain and he know I am serious.

'Oh no. Please, Alexandru. Not the other way. I don't like to do it.'

He means the man at the little Tobacco. Who is old, like sixty. He look like a fat bull. I say to Gogu that he has a hand and that is good for many things. Especially good if the hand can earn him the cigarettes. Gogu look sad. But I laugh. I punch him on the arm and say, it is even more better today as it get him a pastry as well. A Hand of Many Good Talents, I say.

Gogu want to prepare some more. I think he not want to do it. After the food, I want to smoke. So it's time to go.

3

I watch from across the street. The little Tobacco is a street box. The man open quickly. When he see Gogu, he tell him to enter. The man sit down and there is no room for Gogu. I must stay out of the sight and stay down. I have laugh many time at thinking what Gogu must do for the packet. He say he only use his hand. But I think no. Today I not laughing. Maybe because my belly is full. It make me wish to sleep. Maybe it is too hot. Maybe I am tired of the little man with the belly that is like fat bull that has made him lazy. Maybe I like to split his belly. Watch it fall on the street. But maybe it would bounce like a ball and make the cars crash.

Another man with clean, smooth shirt come up. He buy newspaper. The ball belly keep a bored face too. Never knowing that Gogu is busy underneath. One day I change that *fesso*. From bored to scream. But not today. The cigarettes are good. And it is Gogu's hand or mouth. Not mine. I just make sure I don't touch Gogu afterwards. Haha. Is also good for many jokes. For a few good hours of laughing.

This day is becoming very different. Every day is different for my life. Especially for us who not sleep in beds. But some more different again. Not always for good. Now not so good as we have to find somewhere else for the pastries. They are very hard to find. I like the pastry day. The other days are fruit for one day. Bread for another day. Tomato, which is my least best as they are the ones the restaurant do not want. Not fresh like the fruit. This sound bad but not so bad, some thrown away food in the big bin not far from Our Park. Is wrapped in plastic bag and okay inside. Is okay to pull off old salad and sometimes some big chicken or meats forgotten by rich tourists. They are so fat and rich to leave good food in bin. It's okay too for bin because I make Gogu the one to climb in big bin. The more he talk angry, I laugh more and more.

Another good day is pizza day. Is just the bread and the sauce. No cheese or meats. I get them early before the owner start. The baker give us some, only if we not tell others. And come not often. He is good man. Wish for more good mens like him.

'Let us have some fun, Gogu. Let us go to Termini.'

'You said no beg today. You mean to steal?'

'Today no. But maybe if I see easy chance.'

'Alexandru, you are my friend. Please, only if easy chance.' He means about the *polizia*.

'Yes, yes. Just for fun. I want to make laugh with the tourists. That is all for today. It is too hot.'

'Then we go to park for sleep? Gogu tired today.'

'Yes, your hand has been busy. I think your mouth too. It's fantastic you can still talk.'

'Alexandru, you are very cruel boy. Very cruel.'

Before he meant about the time here in the Termini station where I was following a young tourist with a backcase. I opened the case without she knowing. It is almost to laugh at. I not know this but *carabinieri* was following me and I was caught. I struggle that day. They take me to quiet room and gave me a good beat up. They let me go and I walk back to park, which is lucky to be close. Then I did sleep for more than one day, very covered over with bumps and black skin. Gogu help me much then. I still steal sometimes if I cannot get any money for food or cigarettes. But not from Termini. I'm more smart now.

4

Too many peoples everywhere in the Termini station, only half Italiano. I go in and out like motorbike. Gogu follow. I make noise like train. I stop.

'*Stupido*!' I slap him across top of head.

Then we go again. All the peoples with all the money but it is not good. Too much risk. I go to platform two as the clock say train leaving soon. This is best. The tourists are there with their backcase. And suitcase on the wheels. They are looking lost and dumb like animal with surprise in bin. This is good for fun. I swing my arms and walk like a *capitano*, a *grande* man. I lead my assistant to the car number six and go up the stairs to the door. Gogu on the ground. I hang out the door. Two tourists walking past. Man and woman with the backcase.

'Ticket! Ticket!' I say and put out my hand.

They look at me. Thinking. I think too. Come on, little fish. Jump up. But they keep walking. Gogu laugh. I laugh too. I look out over the Termini. I am high. I feel like a real *capitano*. I like it. More tourist coming, with the suitcase on the wheels. Another man, bull belly and woman too.

'Ticket please!' I know some *Inglese*, not much. But this time the man come at me. I smile, hand out.

'Are you the inspector?' he says.

'*Si*. Ticket. Ticket!' I lean out like a monkey.

The man pull back his hand. 'Little young, aren't you? For all that responsibility?'

I no understand the dumb *Inglese*. '*Si*. Ticket!'

The woman says, 'Clive, I really don't think he's genuine.'

I lean out some more but they walk away. 'Please for the ticket! *Per favore!*'

'We'll wait, thank you,' says the woman. Her *fesso* is wrinkled like my bag of balls.

'Ah, *mignotta*,' I say.

Gogu really laugh.

I see now a real target. Three peoples from the Asia. These ones are very easy. Look like parents and the daughter. She only few years younger than us.

'Ticket! Ticket!'

They come at me. This time I do not hang like monkey but straight with the smart face like *capitano*. '*Si*. Ticket please.'

The man give me his ticket. I look at ticket. I look at him. They all looking up at the great Alexandru, Defender of Mankind. This feel good. I wait, hungry for the eyes. Plus Gogu who all give to me their time. I feel like ancient Roma *capitano*, Nero or some thing. The man hold out his hand for the ticket back.

I say to Gogu in Romanian. 'Run, you idiot!' I go into train and run past all the rooms inside the glass with the seats.

Some peoples are there in the seats. The Italianos who know what we are doing and don't care about the dumb tourist. I get to the end and open the door and see the other open door to outside. There is the skinny Asia man. His *fesso* angry like the bull. I did not expect. I run into the next car. I hear the man behind me now, yelling the funny noises of his dumb language. I would laugh if I was not doing the run. He sound like crazy small dog. Yap. Yap.

There is a woman in my front. She is looking at her ticket for the right glass room and seat but look at me now. She lean towards the glass. She cursing me. I have to push past and jump over her suitcase. I keep running out the door again. I run into next train car. Soon I run out of train cars but man now slow because of woman behind. I quick to rip the ticket. Three bits. Then some more. I let them go on the floor. I keep one so he not put together. I am funny. I get to end of the

car. The man is stop to pick the pieces but still yelling the funny noises.
I go to door outside and jump and land like a tiger. Then I run. Gogu
is ahead of the two Asia females who look like lost cats. Gogu wait but
I run to him. And past. He is slow to follow. He is sure to be dumb
some of the time. I hear the man behind me yell his crazy language. I
sure the *carabinieri* or someone will be here soon. I am running past
the tourists who look angry with me. When I get to end of platform, I
see some Termini man with uniform. I can get out before he get me. I
sneak into the people like snake. I slow down so he cannot see me so
good. I don't know where he is as I hide well. Only when I get to
Grande Termini exit. I stop and look. No where to see him now. No see
Gogu also. I could wait. Too much risk. I am careful to cross the road
to McDonalds. Lots of people. Is better to watch.

I want cigarette. Gogu have the cigarettes. I see a man that is young
with backcase smoking. I go to him. I say, '*Scusi*. Cigarette, please.'

'Sure. Here you go, mate.'

I take. He fire up.

'Is good.'

'No worries.'

'Where you from?'

'New Zealand. Auckland.'

'No know this Awk Land. Is good place?'

'Yeah it's all right, hey. Bit different than this place. You from here
then?'

We try to have talk but my *Inglese* not so good. But better than his
Italiano. I say *arrivederci*. I looking all the time for Gogu. But he not
come out. Maybe he got away but I think no. Maybe his turn for the
grande beat-up. Not so good fun. Maybe I give him last bit of ticket,
now in my pocket. Skinny Asia man will be going no place today.

5

I walk around corner to the busy Cargo di Villa Peretti. Around here lots of Syrians and the black African. They homeless too. Too many Syrians now. They say it is because of war but we wish they to be somewhere else because too many peoples begging. They are *stupido*, though, because too many steal and not have the good story like smart Alexandru who has the Grande Sad Story. Here there is a row of the sleeping blankets some inside them. They more sleep during the day as not so safe at night. They do not trust others. They no have good peoples. We have good peoples in Our Park. Maybe I walk past so they can see Alexandru, a *true capitano*, a king of the streets. If they ask how to do this, I do not tell them. Or maybe I tell them something for a cigarette.

I swing my arms and walk slow like true *capitano*. I like this. They look and I look back. They see the fire in my eyes. They know not to make the joke with me or I rip out their eyes and their throat too.

Two girls are talking. One has the back showing and the other can see me. They look like Syrians. This one is ugly like her parents must be brother and sister. I stare hard. Do not stare at the Alexandru, you filthy shit of bear. She nod at her friend and her friend turn around. To look at me. I must slow down. She is different. Her *fesso* is more handsome, even matching to Alexandru's wishes. She is best. Very handsome. I stop and she stare too, but with smile of little girl. Her friend laugh and she laugh too, but still the eyes shine with the want of Alexandru. I know this. I like it. I like her. Her skin like the dark grape. I must talk to her. I hope she speak some Italiano, as I do not know this *bastardo* Syrian.

'*Buongiorno*. I Alexandru. What is your name?'

The other say something but I say, 'I am not talking with you, camel *fesso*. I am talking to the *principessa*…'

The handsome one say, 'Do not talk to my friend this way, you dog! Do you think you're so beautiful?'

Ah, her Italiano is good, good like me, maybe better. 'Not so beautiful as you, *principessa*, but I am great for my name is Alexandru, meaning the Defender of Mankind.'

The ugly one laugh.

'Shut your camel hole. It stinks.'

The ugly one not laughing no more.

The handsome one says, 'You are very harsh with your words. Is this how you are with all womankind?'

'No,' I say. 'Only camel kind.'

This time, I get a laugh from *principessa*. I laugh too as it makes me very happy to see such a smile. Even more beautiful than I could think. The ugly one not smile and walk away. The *principessa* call out her sorrys to camel *fesso* and her name that I not wish to hear.

I take hold of the arm of *principessa* and turn her to me. 'Forget this one.'

'You are very mean.'

'You laugh also. Are you so mean?'

She smile. Again I see the dark brown of the ocean. I want to kiss the *principessa*. Not even Alexandru could expect this wish with girl from Syrian nation. I so pleased I want another cigarette. I ask if she have. She beg me to follow. She take me to her sleeping blanket. I am smart to look around. Sometime handsome girls are used to trap dumb man for the sex and others to take his money. But I can be sure that she is real. She take her cigarettes from under cardboard bed.

'Are you not worry someone steal?'

'We are good here. We look out for each other and not take what not belongs. Sometimes we share for we are like a big family. Sometimes the boys fight, but always make up again.'

I am surprised. I never leave anything at my bed. There is thieves. She takes two cigarettes. Is going to put packet back.

I say, 'No, take the packet,' and, 'Let's go for walk.'

'But I do not know you.' She says this but take the packet.

'I told you. I am Alexandru. And you must be safe with me, more than anyone in Roma. Now tell me your name or I must call you *principessa* always.'

'Yes, you can call me that,' and she laugh again.

My heart is full. I think Alexandru is in *grande* problem.

'Ara is my name.'

'Ara. I like this. We both have A names. This means it is a match.'

'Already you are thinking of a match?' That smile once more.

This time I say nothing more. Alexandru day it is.

6

We are walking on a road. I forget its name. Soon we are at the Piazzale del Brasile. I not notice the cars and bikes and beeps. I am only noticing Ara. I did not think I would ever like Syrian girl. She is telling me about her longest journey ever across the desert on many such transports. There is lots of bad things and scares to young girl. Most when the separate of her mother and little brother who is arrest at the border. It is much more scare than journey of mine, which was very tired with the lots of walking and mountains. The cold. The hard-to-come sleep. But no troubles with peoples.

We see some grass now and make cool to sit on it. She very slim with the legs. I like them. She pretend to forget I see them. She talking more about very hard time when in Roma first. I also remember the very hard time. We gift each other the story. She say to show me tomorrow of where she live when in Roma first. I say good.

The sun will go soon. We have little sleep on nice grass. It is mine now to pretend because it is too hard with sleep next to a *principessa*. I open my eyes a little to see her *fesso* at rest. Most handsome she is. It is like the best of all sunsets. And the best of stars at once.

7

Now we are back near Termini. Is *principessa*'s wish that I join with her for the begging tonight, so we can eat with each other. I am liking this night. I remember the pastry but I thinking it be for the breakfast tomorrow. If the cats not steal yet. I remember Gogu, who could be at the bed. But I cannot go from Ara.

The dark has come and the lights are showing. Many peoples out.

She say, 'I take you to my places. I show you the Syrian way.'

I say Romanian way much better. She say we should go into game with each other: which person bring the most money. I say I would be winner because Defender of Mankind is my name and I not wish to be too hard on little girl. She punch my chest, which hurt. Alexandru get mad. For little moment. Remember the beautiful *fesso*. And say no more for the night. We not play game. I take real thing. And this is to stay with Ara.

We are walking Via Massino D'Azeglio. Street of *ristorante*. She stop in front of tourists on tables. They know she look for the begging and pretend to forget she is there. She open her mouth and sound come, a beautiful voice of the singing. These words I not understand but the song must be Syrian song. It is nice for the ears. Tourists watching now. And listening. Then man come from *ristorante*. He is waiter. He watch a little, with no surprise on *fesso*. I know soon Ara will go because of waiter. She hold out her hand and go with the singing. Move to one table and one across. Her hand is filling with the coins. It is very quick. I am with surprise.

The waiter say, '*Basta! Basta!*'

She get the last coin and follow with the little clap from the tourists. She walking further. I run to her. She show me. She earn much.

'You are good worker,' I say. 'Good with the sounds of singing too.'

'Much better worker than Defender of Mankind?'

I must smile at her smile. '*Si*. Much better with the beautiful singing.'

She smile now.

I say, 'You are real *principessa*. Too much better for Roma streets.'

'Maybe one day I sing on the *televisiono*.'

I think for the first time. 'Maybe you be famous Syrian girl. The first in Italia.' I am serious.

She smile, very proud. I am proud too.

8

Now we sit on step of Shoeman shop. Shoeman come along and tell us to leave.

I say, '*Principessa* here. No shoes for today. Shoeman have holiday.' I laugh.

So I say, 'We eat our food soon and we go.'

He say be quick. He have no customer. We do as long as we want. I am lucky too as girl buy food for me. Specially beautiful girl. She say not worry because being girl is easy than boy to get money.

I know this but I say still, 'Yes you are right.' And then, 'This is good food. A long time for me to have so much.'

We have a big plate with lots of food. I am used to only one slice. Italia slice is big but plate is better. I look to other side of street and see the people there. They are walking with bellies full. Or soon will be full. For this time I am like them. This is very good night. The best for long time. I hope to be more.

Shoeman not get more customers and he give us the bad eye. Then he close the doors for the night. We stay on step talking. Many things, private. Not all wish to say for now.

Is later. Quiet. Tourists off hiding in hotels and such places. I wonder what it is inside. Very good, I think. One day, I will get to such place. Some young peoples are still here on streets. Go to places for the drinking but also get danger with some bad young peoples and gangs around. Some who hate Romanians and maybe Syrian. I say to Ara to go back and she say time for her to go too.

Soon we are back at her street. We get close to her place of sleeping.

A young man is running at me. A black. Angry. He is big and another behind. A brown. He want the hurting of me too. Ara speak in her language but the black are making the waves with the fist. But he not fight Alexandru before. I am fast and I get low and make the fist to his belly. He fall over me and I jump and the roof of my head hit his chin and it make noise like a battle. I have done good but the other one is running at me and I not stop and he fall me to the ground. Fists waving into my *fesso*. Ara is making with screams. I hope she screams for me and not this other two. The black one is now to come back and hold my arms. I make like a bull but Ara is telling me to be okay. That every peoples is okay. And I think nobody hitting me now. I stop and the one black and one Syrian are coming off me.

'Why are you make with the fighting of Alexandru? I make no war with you.'

The black one is rubbing his *fesso* and is worried for the broke of bones. I not sure. He may be lucky.

The Syrian boy is same age. He say he only worry for Ara for she is like sister and they take care of her.

I say, 'You only want her for the singing and the good money.' I think I shall want to fight. I do not like this one or the black one.

Ara put her hand on Syrian boy shoulder. 'No, this is my friend. We are like family here. I tell you this. They are only worried for me.' She look at boy now. 'It is okay. This is my new friend. This is Alexandru.'

'We didn't know where you went. You didn't say to us.'

'I know. I am sorry. I was having a good day and forgot to tell. I wasn't far and I was okay. It's good you worry.' She smile and shake his hair.

I wish she shake my hair.

'Alexandru, I must go now.'

I not know the words to make now. I was hope to try to give this Syrian *principessa* my lips to be with hers. But this two *cafone* will not leave for my chance.

'Maybe I see you tomorrow?' she say.

'*Si si. Bene.* Good thought.' I begin to walk, as I cannot think any words. The words in my head. All too many.

'Okay. *Ciao*! Thanks for the fun day!'

'*Ciao*. Thanks for cigarettes!' I wave. I walk away.

She had bought the cigarettes after the pizza and give me some. I walking to Giardini Piazza Vittorio. My home. Wishing I had said more words than thanks for cigarettes. This only wrong things in this day that was *perfecto*. I hope Gogu is in bed, so I tell him all about this beautiful Ara who so close to me. I have never seen until this day. Sometimes the strange things is life.

9

As one hand is light, the other is heavy. I find my bed empty. My pastry is taken. There is no picture of Gogu any place. I can wait only. The sleep does not come. The mosquitos bad this night. I can sleep without them most nights. All thoughts are flow through my head. Beautiful Ara. The food on the step. The hit of the black man. The run through the train. The girl singing. The bull belly man in Tobacco box. All too much in my head. For hours.

Now Alexandru on platform watching Gogu run through train. Many *carabinieri* are running behind. But Gogu go too slow. I yell but Gogu not hear through glass. *Carabinieri* catch and beat him many times. Black man and Syrian boy hold me and I cannot run to stop *carabinieri*. Now I am in glass in street. I see Tobacco box and belly man, who open door and Ara go in. I cannot move still and she go down. Belly man smile at me. I know what she does. Lips of beauty on dirty *cazzo*. I scream. I want to kill him with my fist. But I can do nothing. He open the door and Ara fall out in pieces like glass. She is broken. I cry. This is strange. I have not cry for too long. I cannot remember. I am free. I sit up. I am in park. It's very light. I have sleep very late. My *fesso* is wet. Tears. I think I cry for real. I clean the tears, before some people see me. I up and walking to spring fountain. Same old friends with greetings. Surprise at my *fesso* which is down and looking at ground. I go to water of fountain and make wet my *fesso* and hair. I take walk in middle of park to way out. I don't care for the walk under trees like always. I want to look for the freshness of Ara.

I make quick through the streets. Still drying with the wet on my clothes. I go different street to keep from Termini distance. Maybe *carabinieri* looking for me. Maybe Gogu tell where I live. I did not think of this. Thinking too much of *principessa*. Maybe Gogu barter good room to be his. To give up Alexandru to *polizia*. Gogu too easy. Not strong like me. I take the beat-up and be quiet. Maybe time is come. Give up Giardini Piazza Vittorio. Maybe for long time. I ask Ara if she wish for me to live with her. Then I see someone wave across street. It is Ara. I am now very happy. I not think of anything. I make like a snake across the road.

'I saw you! I've followed you. Why are you going all back and up the streets?' She is smiling hard.

I see Syrian boy and black man not far but pointing and laughing.

I lift my fist. 'You want to try more? This time I leave your *fesso* like smash tomato!'

'Don't look at them,' she say and touch my shoulder. Her touch is nice. 'Come. Let's go. I take you to the place. We take Metro.'

'I no have money. Is hard to past inspector.'

'I have coins for us. I will buy ticket. No problem.' She about to go but I stop. 'What is wrong? Don't you want to see?'

'Yes. Very much. But no like girl to spend money all times.'

'You mean for the boy to pay? Ha ha. This is very old-fashioned Romanian boy. It is easier for girl on streets to get the money. No problem. One day, when you have money, you pay, okay?'

I do not speak but we go. I not so sure today. Today is different. But I know that nobody laugh at Alexandru. Syrian and black. I get them when they not ready.

10

Ara standing with me by doors on Metro. She talking much. I am listening. I am proud to be by this girl. The train is stopping. We are at the Ostiense Stazione. I follow her. We go up to exit. She walk quick. Nice to watch her legs and *sedere*.

She say, 'There are many places here. I show you my old place. Maybe after I take you to some old platforms and hiding places. See if there is anyone left. Maybe some new people from my country. Is this okay?'

'If you like.'

'Yes, I would like this. My people still come from my land. It is still bad there.'

I only know park and Roma. I forget much.

We come outside. The clouds hide the sky. This place is big. More than Termini. We walk some minutes. She take me to *buco*. This is covered by round metal. This away from big entry of station. Easy to open without eyes watch. I look inside and see cement not far.

'Is this really here?'

'*Sì.* Let's go in.' She go in, not far.

I follow. It is low but step down to more space.

'Let's pull this back, but not all the way. It's heavy and there's only two of us.'

We lift our hands, side to side. I very close. I smell her. She smell good. I want to kiss her very much. We pull that metal, almost close, so the light is shorter. But I not move. I see her. She watch me too. This is right time. I put my hands on her arms. I pull her to me. I push my lips on her lips. They are very nice. The kiss. Ah, *principessa*. The most beautiful in the world. Her lips is opening. She is wanting to eat my lips. She touch my chin, pull down. She want me to open lips too. I do this. Now her lips fit into mine. This is very nice. I am trying to follow. Now I am hot. I pull her onto my body, which is stiff for her. I want to pull out my little man. I want to push all on her skin. Push my little man in her beautiful hole.

She push me back. 'Come. I want to show you where we live.' She pull away from my hands.

But I don't wish to let her go. I don't mind for where she live now. I want only Ara.

'Come on. We do no more,' she say. 'I am a good Syrian girl. We only kiss.' She pull out of my hands and go around me like little ant.

'Nobody see us here.'

She go under long pipes into wall. 'See? I sleep here. My friends also sleep along here.'

I don't think my little man have fun today. 'It not nice here. Bad smell.'

'*Si*. I forget. But you forget the smell after not too long. Come on, I show you other place.' She go out from pipe which is warm for water. She go into tunnel, like funny little rat.

I look at her *sedere*. I could push my little man on it and nobody see. Push into any hole. I like to make mine for fun. But she not like me if I make her do it. Then no more of the nice kiss. And the smile to Alexandru. I will keep to trying. I think her hole wet like fountain for Alexandru. But maybe later.

I follow her. We go into other rooms of cement like footpath. Some with lights, others no light. I hear water. It smell bad too. But much room for homeless people. She say that with some cold nights in winter one hundred peoples in this room. Many kids like her, who come from Syria. All kids and not many adults. I say not very nice with so many peoples and smell. But warm in winter. Better than park. So maybe this is not bad.

'Where are all the peoples?' My voice come back from all the walls. Sound like many Alexandrus.

She say, 'One day we was caught by the *carabinieri* and lots of important peoples come. They took all the children and some adults. I not sure where they go, but some say the children looked after in shelter. I do not know because I made the escape. Maybe shelter might be better but maybe they now be sent back to Syria. I no want to go back again. Too bad there with much war. Better to be here on streets with my friends.'

'*Si.* Syria sound like place of shit.'

'Oh no, you do not understand. It is beautiful. It is my country. But it is bad now. Maybe one day I go back and it be better.'

'Maybe I come with you. You have Alexandru to be your nice friend for long time like husband.'

She smile. Like a *principessa.* The best. 'I think only for today. Too young for husband. Maybe boyfriend only.'

'Boyfriend? This is it! *Si. Perfecto!*'

'Boyfriend. *Si.* Okay.'

Now I pull her to me and kiss some more. Is very nice and special in the rooms under Roma. Very special to remember. For all times to come.

11

There is much bang. Very noisy. Room is now dark.

'Somebody's closed the gate!' she say. I can tell the frighten in her voice.

'It's okay. We push up. You know where to find?'

'Uh, *si*. Most of the time it was dark before. But someone have candles then.'

I find her hand and take. 'Take me there.'

She hold my hand. I can tell she is find her way with other hand.

'Here. It is here.'

I touch up to round metal. Hole. Metal. Door. Some word, I cannot make. It is warm from day. 'Okay, we push together okay? *Uno, duo, tre*…push!' I give everything.

She is too but metal not moving.

'We must try more,' I say.

'No. This is not right. It should open. Something must be on it. A person.'

All the bad thoughts come to my head. The *carabinieri* have seen us. Or the *stazione* peoples. Watched the metal to watch if homeless peoples come back. Now we are like chicken in cage. Prison. Ready to eat.

'We must be caught. What will we do?' she say.

She put her arms around my belly. Her *fesso* in my skin. Her eyes flick with hairs on my skin. It feel funny.

She say, 'I don't want to go back. Is too bad. I wish to die in Italia.' Her eyes now wet.

I am not used to this crying of girls. I should be man now.

'We try again. Then if closed, we hide in rooms down here to see if peoples come. Then try some more. They will not find us. Alexandru make sure, okay?'

She breathe in the nose. Sniffy sounds. *Molto.*

'Come. Try again.'

She let go of me. We touch the metal.

'*Uno, duo, tre…*push!'

The round metal go up straight. Yes! I push back and the light fall all over us. We close our eyes until the light agrees. Very good. Then I look all ways. I see no peoples.

'Maybe some people just walk on.' I lift to help *principessa* up. Her *fesso* is scared like kid. I like it.

We close the plate.

A man come at us. Tall with hair falling off head. Smoking cigar in mouth's corner. 'Find anything down there?'

I look at him with bad eyes. He have cracks in his *fesso*. He ugly like old cement street. I no like.

I say to Ara, 'Let us go now.'

'Wait on,' he say. 'You're not living down there, are you? Because those immigrant *bambini* got into a lot of trouble. You're not immigrants, are you? Because you do look like it.'

I watch his *fesso*. He look to me. He think he smart more than me. I no like him. *Cafone.*

I push him heavy with two hands and he go back but not fall. 'You lucky I no fist you in mouth! Break cigar!' He very lucky, but soon not so lucky.

'Hey, hang on. I'm a friend. I wouldn't tell the *carabinieri*, though some people might. Not me. I can help.'

She say, 'We don't want help. We are okay. *Vaffanculo.*'

He laugh. 'Ha ha ha. I like this girl. She quick with the fuck-off insult.'

I say, 'Maybe you listen.'

'Don't you want to earn some money?' he say. 'It's good money.'

'Not for you. No,' I say.

'It's not with me. You'll be working with someone else. It's a one-off job. Very good money.'

'How much?' she say.

'I pay fifty euro up front before you even do the job, to prove my good intentions.'

'I don't like,' I say.

'Listen. Fifty first, then after, another hundred. It's a very good deal. A lot of euro for you.'

'Is a lot,' she say.

'*Si,*' I say. 'But I don't know.'

The man say, 'If you don't want it, I'll find someone else.'

She look at me. 'That's one hundred and fifty euro. That's um…'

'Seventy-five each,' he say.

I no believe him.

But Ara say, 'Yes, that's true. Seventy-five.' She is good with the learning. She must have the school. 'Seventy-five each? I never see this much in my hands.' She look at the man ugly *fesso*. 'What is this job? When is it?'

'All it takes is a couple of calls. We could do it tomorrow night. I will meet you at seven in the evening. I pay you fifty euro, because I am a good man, and instruct you from there. You do the job, come back to me, and you'll be a lot richer by the time you go to sleep, wherever it is you sleep. Not down there, you say.'

I put my hand to Ara. I no wish him to know anything. 'Tell him nothing.'

He say, 'It makes no difference to me.'

She say, 'How do we know you still pay us a hundred after? You should pay before.'

His cigar has gone off. He take it out. 'No. If I pay you upfront you won't do the job. But I'm a fair man and that is why I pay you fifty first. But listen, if you don't want the job, then you piss off. There's plenty of others I can find.'

She put her hand on my arm. I thought she wish for kiss, which is strange time. But she take me away from man and whisper to me. 'Even fifty is good. If we don't like job, we will run.'

I nod. 'I listen to you, Ara.'

We go back to man and I say, 'Okay, we do job. Now what is job?'

'Tomorrow, my friend. I will tell you all tomorrow.'

12

We are out on street, not far from the home park of mine. Back to where I like. Not at Ostiense, which I do not like. Ara no like much too, no more, I think. She no go look for friends. She make talk with other Syrian who live there but she not know friends from before. She is too sad, the thoughts there. Now we think of the job. I have ten-euro note and twenty-euro note in my pocket. This is good. Ara is with twenty-euro note. I will give some of mine so I will be fair. We now wait for the dark which is near. Ara is talking but I no hear. I say to her I do hear but I no want to. Tired with the words. Ara is *principessa* but she makes too many words for one day.

I look with the hard eyes at the Italiano with us now. He is old to me, but not too much. His *fesso* is hard with too many fighting. I think maybe he once very bad. Maybe good with the fight. I think if I fight him, I win. He no talk to us but I am sure he with the money. I want to ask but still I am not sure of his job.

'Are you listening to me?' She hit in my side.

'What are you…?'

'I say to you, if you listen…' and she come closer, '…when you kiss, you should keep your eyes shut!'

'Hey, why you say this? I kiss good!' Stupid *mignotta*.

'Yes, but I can feel you watching too and this is strange.'

'You strange. Maybe you like to kiss him. The Italiano with no words.'

'Don't be this way. I only like you. You know this.'

'Humph. Maybe not. No like the kiss.'

'I do! Just close your eyes.'

'But then I no see you. Why I want to do that?'

She smile and hug me. This girl, I cannot understand. I try not to think and only think of the job. Job is too simple. He best to give me the money or I make his cigar very hot up his *culo*. If he give me the money, this is good. Maybe I do more job for him. Maybe get more money. More jobs. Maybe I find room somewhere. And get Ara to come and sleep in my bed. Real bed. Soft. The white sheets. Pillow. Two if I have the money. Then I sure that Ara take my little man in her little secret hole. I like it.

'We could go now,' she whisper.

I say I do not understand what she say.

She say, 'We have fifty euro. We could have much fun tonight. Eat and drink what we want. And still have money for cigarettes tomorrow.'

I hold her back so Italiano not hear. Stupid girl. I not let go of her. 'You do not understand my dream. This is only first job. We make lots of money. We…'

Italiano is coming at me.

'Quiet now,' I whisper but girl turn around. *Stupido*.

The man nod to street. Time to leave. His eyes say he hate me and her. Like we are *stupido* cat in street. But he not know me. I am smart. If he want to fight me, I fight him first. Real good. I forget the money. Alexandru come first. Money is second. No. Money is after. Ara is second. It is dark now. Streets have the many peoples which is every day. Many tourists too. It still warm. Only when cold not many tourists, but always some.

The man walk first. We follow. We walk past *ristorante*. People at table. Eat the good food. Talking with all the languages. *Inglese* and others. One day I sit here too. With all the money. They say in their eyes they not see me. The dirty street boy. But inside they scared of me. They have different *fesso* but always with the same look.

We are crossing the road and car almost hit me so I have to stop. Car hit many peoples in Roma. Not care if homeless young like me. We go again. Man is on corner, leaning on the wall. The man with the job for us. Good. I think he not be real. But he is here. Good for the more money.

Look to next street, which is smaller than this one. When I get to him, he point at shop. I know this place. It has man from India or such place who own it. I buy cigarette here before. He has India wife who sometime work there. Shop always open, even siesta time. Sometime I go past and see little kids play there. Two. The India kids speak good *Italiano*. Better than father. And maybe me too.

'This shop?' I say.

'*Sì*. Hurry now.'

I look to Ara. She look to me for answer.

It is only shop, so I say, 'Okay?'

She say nothing. But I see she think okay too. I want the money, so I think we be quick. I look for cars better this time. I walk across small road to front of shop.

I look to Ara. I touch her *fesso*. 'New time for us.'

She nod. I turn and go in shop. It is bright. I see the watches and flashies on right. Many rows. False for tourist. On left, hats, T-shirts and many junk for tourist again. India man work now. No wife or kids. Maybe out back, I don't know.

'Hey, India man! You should not be working in this shop!'

This India man take job from man who give us the job. His shop. Some story I forget. Italiano man say to us we have to make mess. But easy to clean. I take off the hats and throw them. They go through air like plane. Flying hat birds. Very funny to look. Ara laugh.

'Hey! What are you doing? Get out of my shop!'

Ara take the flashies with one arm and push onto floor. It make big sounds but not many break. Some. I laugh.

India man stand up. 'You crazy boy! I remember you. I know your face! I call the *polizia*!'

He have many cigarettes behind. I want them. 'Hey, give me one of those. That one. Give me that one!'

Now his *fesso* get mad.

'I won't hit you. I want cigarettes only.'

'Then you should find other shop!'

I say, 'This not your shop. This is other man's shop. You know this. Don't lie!' I say I won't hit but if he try to hit me I hit first. I no hate India man. His kids funny. I like.

I hear bang and look. Ara have pull over the tall metal holder. The many magazines all over floor. She make mess very big. I laugh. She good.

'You terrible shit! You will not get away with this. I have *videosorvegliata*!' India point to camera video in corner. Is this bad? Can this camera get me with *carabinieri*?

'Bangladeshis out! *Italia* for Italianos!'

This is not India voice. Not Ara. Not I. I see man walk quick in. With black jumper over his head so no see *fesso*, only eyes. But I know his clothes. This is Italiano man with us, who give job. He have something in his hand. A long can which sprays. He next to me. He lift can. He lift other hand and flick a small flame. He push at India man and spray. It make big fire and splash all over India man. I jump back far. India man scream like cat I see on fire one day, when kids play game. Not nice. But this very bad. So very bad. I can not believe but India man run into wall, which go on fire too. I move away quick. Ara scream. She is scared. With the man with can and jumper on head run out. And new scream, which is India wife at back door. She see me. Then look to husband, who fall to floor. Scream like wild pig. I can not look. Smell bad too. Very bad. Too late for him. Must go now and run to Ara and pull her to door as I think *carabinieri* will come and I fall on mess on floor. Ara pull me up now.

We go through door. Some people are coming to look and they maybe see us but we run up street. We go very fast and I get to corner and almost run on big road. I do a bit and car beep and almost are hit. I go back and go past car and we run more on street, run fast. I think this very bad. Get away quick but Ara not as quick in long street. I think to maybe run away. I like *principessa*. So I go slow so she get up with me. I go with her but have to stop at next corner. My breath very dry and heart very fast too. I look for quiet place to go. All is busy with peoples and tourists to Roma. This is bad. Ara is almost with the tears. Peoples look at her. And me too. With the very strange eyes.

'You must calm!' I say. 'You must be like every day so peoples no look, okay?'

'Okay,' she say, but she not look like every day. Her *fesso* with the frighten.

I frighten too. This very bad.

Now there is siren. *Carabinieri* to the India place. For real. We can no go to park of mine. Or to friends of Ara. *Carabinieri* will see the camera video. Maybe know how to find us.'

'We must hide,' I say.

'But my friends! I must see them! I want to see them!'

'We cannot make the risk. We must hide.'

'No, no. But we didn't do anything!' She take my arm strong. 'We didn't do anything!'

'Shh! *Stupido* girl.'

Peoples looking. I see many. Maybe they know. Maybe not. Maybe they tell later.

'Follow me.' I take her arm.

I get off big street and go into Piazza, this one Zingari which go to small street. Maybe go all the way to Colosseo. No tourists now but in day, too many. This could be idea. Good place to hide with tourists for Romanian boy and Syrian girl. Maybe good idea. Maybe sleep in Palantino tonight. Jump over fence and sleep with the old Roman. I sleep here before. Not so bad but many cats. I happy to sleep with them tonight if *carabinieri* not find me. And Ara. And big trouble. To blame for India man. Very bad. And very very bad for India man. The screams of a pig. The smell of meat. I will not forget this. Forever.

13

I still not sleep. My back hurt on the ground, but I no care so much. *Principessa* head on my chest. This is first time I sleep with girl. I like. I am on grass under little tree. I still see stars which I make sure I see, like in park. I like the stars. My mama tell me they are angel souls watch on me. This before Mama die of the sickness. Before I go to uncles, who hit me too much. If I was this size now, I fuck him good. But too small and must run away. I not know which angel soul is for me so I must always see stars on me. I think Mama there too. Maybe I have two angel souls. I think if Ara have one, we have three, or maybe not but if she with me then okay.

Ara make the bad dream sound. She make it before.

I touch her *fesso* but she no wake. She make strange sound. I put my hand on her mouth. I not know if guard man here or not. 'Only bad dream. You are with Alexandru. It is okay.'

Her eyes big with the bad dream. But she see me, the real Alexandru and stop with the moving. I let go of her mouth and she breathe big.

'Oh, it was very terrible,' she whisper.

'What happen in that dream?'

'Dream? I mean the man. The burning man. It was terrible.'

'*Si*. Very bad. I not see this before. I only see man cut with knife and peoples shot with the guns.'

'I've seen that too. I also see bomb happen on the road, just after, and there were all different people with bits on the road in different places. I saw a dog come up and take a bit. Hungry dog. I saw a woman too. She was half-old with one leg and one arm. She called out for

Abdullah, over and over, but too much blood come out of her. Then she go quiet for good.'

'I saw a boy who making the complain to men who take us over border. They shot him in the leg. He fall down and they shoot one place over a lot and his leg fall off. They pick up his leg. He look funny. I laugh.'

Ara look at me with the bad eyes.

I say, 'He was very bad boy. He make people dead. It was better that way, I think.'

'It was the scream. The scream was so terrible.'

'The boy did not scream. He yell mad about his leg and they shot him more. I don't think he know the pain. Strange, no?'

Ara stand. I still on the ground. I look up at her. She look like she in with the stars. She is of the stars. Angel soul girl.

'Do you believe he is dead? He must be dead. Why did he die?'

'I tell you this. India man take shop from man who give us job.'

She no understand. 'Why did we have to mess up the shop if he was to die?'

I say, 'Maybe to give him lesson.'

'It's not fair. I would not do this job if I knew what would be done.'

'Me too,' I say. 'The Italiano man is lucky I no see him after or he would be burning man too. Maybe I go look for him at Ostiense.'

'Do you think we can find him? Do you think we could tell the *carabinieri* about him?'

'I think no. They no like young immigrants. We will make to leave Italia. Or be lock in the cage. No. We must hide some places very good.'

'Prison? No. I won't go there.' Ara walk away.

'Where you go?'

'I have to go with the pee pee.'

I no not what to say, so I say nothing. I look at the wall that is little. That is broked. This is from old concrete. This is old Roman wall. Why do tourists want to see old and broked and not much? Here when

Pantheon is good and strong and full. I do not understand this tourists. I think they must be very dumb and stupid. Where they live must be very dumb peoples.

I lay down again and look at stars. I wonder if India man have angel star. Maybe he is star now, but only in India. I do not know. I never learn many things from Mama. She dead too quick for my growing up. I no go to school, only very short time. I know only little reading and numbers. I cannot remember. I think Alexandru not know these things that normal *bambini* know. Like what is good and what is bad. But I know many thing other *bambini* not know. The way to live in country and city with no adults. The way to live on the streets and parks. This is good thing to know.

Ara is here. 'I been thinking…'

'In the pee pee?' I smile.

She smile. 'Yes, funny boy. I think the Italiano man ask us to do this job so that the camera only see our faces and not the man. We would never be getting this one hundred euro. The *carabinieri* only looks for us now.'

I stand up. '*Si*. The camera video only see us. *Bastardo*. He play big game with us. I no like this. I no like him. I think we go to Ostiense. Alexandru very good with bottle that broken with the edges. I play good game with his belly and his *fesso* and much blood like fountain. I cut his heart and make him to eat. *Fanculo*! I do this day!'

<h1 style="text-align:center">14</h1>

We now at the water spring in the Foro with the Old Place of Romans. It is dead city. But already the alive ones, the tourists, have come like flies to pick clean over the body with the camera. Tomorrow they be gone and new ones come. But they are all the same flies.

The water is good and cold. We wash the clothes as good to look like tourists. This is Ara idea.

We walk about the drying but still with the strange eyes at us. All about the pointing and the click click and the camera and phone. Peoples are very strange.

'I wish we have one. Then we be real tourist.' I say.

Ara grab my arm.

I smile. 'This is good idea. No?'

We walk around with the pretend point and the laugh. But still they look at us. I know what I must need. I see a good time for camera. We get the money for the stealing. I do not steal much but sometime it is no other thing to do. To get food I must do this.

I see two old peoples. Very old like dead that walk. They sit on corner, drink water from bottle. I go from behind. Camera is next to man when he drink. Stupid man. Very slow is best. I take real slow. He know nothing. Now, camera mine. Tourist dumb.

We only walk quick. We go to exit that go to Colosseo with the big thing over the top. I know not what this thing is. Big white thing. 'Ah, Arco!' I say. I remember. 'This is Arco. I like this.' It is good shape.

'Keep walking,' she say.

I see she is worry for the exit man look at us. I smile at him. I hold the camera. My camera now. '*Ciao, ciao!*'

Exit man. His *fesso* stay the same and we go out. We go with all the peoples. I look at the tourists. Now I pretend to do what they do with the point and click click. We walk in and out. All around. Colosseo. With the fighting mens from old days. Romans. Colosseo. It look good. But this be much more good if they make it all to finish. With roof. *Stupido.*

I say, 'I think we go to Metro. To go to Ostiense.'

She no look good with me. 'No. This is a bad idea. Maybe *carabinieri* looking for this bad man. I think it's better if we go to a new place.'

'You no like Alexandru's idea?'

She look at me. 'I would like to get this man also, but we must hide. I think this is best. For some time. Maybe later, we come back and get him. But not now.'

'They see our *fesso* with the camera video.'

'*Si,*' she say. She is smart, this Syrian *principessa.*

'Maybe we go and sell camera now.'

I look around. I hear some peoples with the bad words at the other. Man with woman. Maybe husband with wife. They have suitcase with the wheels but look bad from the inside.

'How do I know where it is?' he say.

'Well, if you'd brought the frigging map like I told you instead of leaving it on the bed, you'd know exactly where it is, wouldn't you?'

'Jesus Christ, Christine! Let's just get a fucking cab.'

'Then we'll be too early. I told you. I'm not waiting around a train station.'

'Every second person isn't a fucking pickpocket.'

I am close and I say, 'You want to go to station? Is this the Termini?'

The woman say, 'Ah Geoff, he looks like one of those…'

'Yes, actually,' the man say. 'Do you know the way?'

'I take you. It's okay. No problem.'

'Really? That's fantastic.'

'Geoff?'

I see the wife who want to go away from me but the man who is

Geoff no want to listen. I know. She with the lumpy fat and all the perfume. He want to follow me quick to make her more bad. This is funny. I like.

She is with the noise and complain all the way. She is *mignotta*. So I give her the smile. I look at her belly much. She must have much money to have all the food. I have the laugh inside of me. Ara not know what I do this. She do not like *mignotta* too. But I like because everyone follow Alexandru.

We are in Termini. It is busy with the peoples and tourists. I hope no people see me who knew me. Young and immigrants know Alexandru here. Homeless Italiano also.

I ask Geoff what is the train he want.

He look and say, 'Sorrento.'

I show him the board and point. I say that is there. Platform 11. I remember this platform. I did good.

He look at wife and say to me, 'Excellent job, buddy.'

She look away. But I like it.

'How much do I owe you?' He pull out his money.

I look at the money. I could grab and run and he could do nothing. I am too fast. I say, 'Ah, okay. I have train too.'

'Huh? Look here, buy a new T-shirt. Looks like you could do with one.'

The lumpy *mignotta* say, 'Geoff, what are you doing? Don't give them money. It's probably a scam.'

He give me a ten-euro note. 'He helped us out. What's the problem? Thank you, my friend.'

I say, 'This is good. *Grazie mille.*'

'No problem, buddy.' He look to wife. 'Cheaper than a taxi. Worth it just to keep you quiet the whole way. I should pay him double.'

They go away still with the bad words at the other.

Ara say, 'What are you doing?'

I smile. 'I have twenty and ten now. This is good, *sì?*'

'Five of it is for me. Remember that?'

I did forgot. '*Sì*. I know this.'

'I don't understand. I thought you said Termini is a bad place for you.'

'Is true. But you said you want to go to new place. We can do this. This is place for new place. We go to platform 11. We must be quick. If someone see me, is bad for both.'

15

There are many eyes. Many tourists but many Italiano. I have camera I take from dumb tourist. I think Italiano know I am not tourist. Best to get on train. It is here. The blue one. Engine is on but not go yet. We walk in cars to number four. I see the tourists. Look with the lost in their eyes for their ticket. No time for the funny now.

'Get on here,' I push at Ara's back.

'But we don't have a ticket. I don't want to get caught.'

'Be quiet, *stupido*. Hurry.'

She go up. I follow.

It is a long train with many glass rooms with seats inside. Not like the train for small places. So I think it best we stand in hallway.

She say, 'Where do we sit?'

All seats has number on the ticket.

'Ticket we no have. I no want to sit because someone could have right seat and get angry. Conductor man find us.'

'What will we do? Please. I think we should go somewhere else.' Ara is lost. Worry on *fesso*. Maybe with the scared inside.

Bad time. Maybe the stars not watch us this day.

I take her hand. I say, 'We cannot be in Roma. For us Roma too bad now. And for long time. You know this. I will take you to place is better. And free.'

I want to look at her and protect for long time. Is possible. I want to push Ara down to a ball and put in my pocket. Or carry her like little dog. I put my hand on hair. I wish to kiss everywhere. I think Ara be mine until I die. Is best I die before her. I no wish to see her die. I don't think we get old. We are too poor. Too much immigrant. Always die. Or forget about. No good place for us. Maybe die together. I think yes. I think this they call the Love.

'I'm so nervous,' she say. 'I think we will be caught. And they will say it is our fault that the man was killed. We will be shot. I know it.'

'Shhh. Be quiet now.'

Someone is getting on. I lean and give Ara the hug so they won't look too much. It is Italiano woman with glasses for sun and much perfume, *puzzo*. She go past.

'I want to go to *bagno*. Toilet.'

I kiss her cheek and next cheek. 'Okay, lovely. It's okay. We will be okay. Alexandru look after you. I make this wish for you.' I take her through glass door to door. *Bagno*.

She point. 'Is this it?'

'*Si*.' I smile as she go.

I make big puff. I am not scared. No. But I wish to go. Train not ready. I say I look after Ara. I do this or die. No peoples must want to stop me. Or very bad for them. I no problems to make peoples die. I ready to die this day. I take Ara too. Save her the worry. She not be scared. She not know. I be quick. I do this for Love.

I turn to look at other door. There is gap of stones, one track and other train but no platform. No peoples allowed here. Only platform on other side of train. There is man clean the paint shapes made by the young. He clean to take off the train. His clothes too big. He look *stupido*. He is young too. He just there. He turn to look at me. He must know I watch him. His *fesso*. I know well. Gogu. Ha ha, Gogu. His one eye is seeing me. He know its Alexandru. His speaking and nodding and making it with the big happiness.

'Sshhh,' I say. But he no listen. I try the door. I open it.

'Alexandru! It is very good to see my friend. It is!'

'Sshhh. Come here!' I drop down to stone. I stand and grab him.

He try to hug, still making with the talk too loud. I put my hand on his mouth to shut the words and turn him and put my arm around his neck. Stupid Gogu. He try to finish me. I cannot have him to see me. I pull back hard and put my foot and push him down onto stone by this train so no peoples can see.

'Be quiet, *stupido fanculo*.'

Lucky this train be empty. He has the uniform of Termini. He not the same. He is like Italiano now. Not Romanian. Not Gogu. This can not be like before. I with Ara now. Ara come back soon. I pull hard again and his neck go with my arm. He kick the stones and want to push me off. But I cannot do this now. I on top and too strong for him. I tell him quiet, I must look after Ara. I no wish for this now. It is too bad for Gogu. Ara and Alexandru. She is *principessa* of my life. She is this day. She is tomorrow. Ara is Tomorrow. Gogu is gone. I do this for her.

He slow down. He will stop soon. Like a cat I saw with older kids in our park. They put the shirt on its head. I only watch but I learn many things. I was boy then. And now Gogu is like the stones. No move. Silly boy is Gogu. But he not too easy to fit with the stones. If I put him under train, I could. But when train go, some peoples see. And stop the train. I look this way and that way. Only trains and stones. I crawl like cat to look at this train. See peoples inside glass. I quick crawl back. Too many peoples. Only one way to do. I go back to door and go up.

'There you are,' she say. 'What have you been doing? You took a pee pee? You couldn't wait?'

I grab her arms. 'We have no time. You must help me. Some bad has come.'

'What do you mean? What bad?'

I put my hand on her mouth, the hand that also on Gogu's mouth. I take her to door and open quick. I beg her to look down, quick and close. She see Gogu. Her eyes are big. I wish to make words and the shaking. Some people is coming up the door. Shit. I hug Ara and make pretend like other time. But now I feel her shake. This time the big scared is inside her. I whisper to her what we must do but quick, quick,

quick. We do this or die for both. The only thing I pretend to forget is not tell Ara who is Gogu. He is only train man who cleans. This must be secret. This is end. Goodbye, friend.

95

16

Ara is at *bagno* door. I wait out. To protest. A man is come to get in. 'Please to use other door, *signore*. This is problem with toilet. Very bad. Much shit.'

Man curse. He dumb tourist. But there is other *bagno* in train. He lucky I no fist his *fesso*.

I hear Ara as I pull Gogu along floor. I am strong. And this time, I am very quick.

17

Train is going along. I am shut in *bagno*. With two peoples that know Alexandru. One girl who cry but quiet. One boy is quiet, no cry. I do not wish for this way. This is very bad for all. Only wish now to be out of Roma. Roma is *grande. Molto grande.* It is time to be out. I wait for some thing I know is come soon. And soon it is come. Some people at door. If I no answer, people get conductor. This no good. I must do this. I show Ara to be quiet. But she know. I open door. Slow and little gap just for my head. It is a Lady of Holy in the long black clothes. Special Lady. I see this Lady of Holies in Roma. The mans too. Some days many Italiano peoples come to see the *Grande* Holy Pope and this place, Vatican. 'I sorry, Lady Holy. Toilet is *finito*. Very bad with the *puzzo*.'

'Oh dear.'

'I clean. Long time.'

'I see. Poor boy. This is not a good job for a young man, is it? I suppose someone must do it.'

'Ah, I sorry. No good with words.' She speak too quick.

She nod and go away. I close door. I feel good I get lady to go but Ara no happy. She only look at wall.

18

It is long time before I be out of city. We are out of Roma. Many grass that is yellow and rocks and the place for farms. It is good to be out. I make Ara go to hallway.

She come back quick. 'The conductor is coming!'

This not good. I knew he come soon. Okay to get on train. Always conductor come somewhere. Ara come back in. I can talk around conductor but not with Gogu here. I close *bagno* door. And wait.

Ara is shaking. I can see easy. I do not shake. We are catched. Or not. No have to shake.

The door is try to open. I say nothing. Ara hide in corner like before. The door is knocked.

'*Salutore!*'

'Ah, *scusi*. Just checking. Have I seen your ticket?'

'No. I have *grande* problem with stomach. Bad salami. *Molto*.'

He laugh. 'Okay.' Then quiet.

I look at Ara but she no look at me.

'That was quick, yes? Bad salami is funny, no?'

She no look again.

'I know you are not happy with this here.'

Gogu is turn down so she no see his eyes. I could not close his eyes. He is dead but still make me smile with the one eye. Gogu not so bad. He only make Alexandru journey bad. Bad for him. But this only way. Gogu no need to work for Termini peoples.

'You wish to be in the prison? *Si*? If I no do this, you be with *carabinieri*. They like little Syrian girl. They take your clothes away. They do the thing to you. All of them. With the little mans in the hole under your legs. You like? Also in the poo poo. *Si.* Italiano mens like the poo hole. After, then take you to Syrian land. You want this?'

She say nothing. She no look at Alexandru.

'Ah, silly girl. Maybe you like many dirty Italianos in your hole.'

'Shut up. Do not speak about me like this.'

'You no like Alexandru in your hole? You think you too better than Alexandru?'

'I can't believe this.'

'Maybe you have no hole. Italiano make hole for you. Many all together. *Si. Molto fanculo.*'

I go to window and pull down. I no wish to see her *fesso* no more. I see grass. I see farm fence of stone. This good enough place. I go to door. I open. I look in hallway. I go out and shut door. This quiet but must be quick. I open door to outside. Very wind and noise of train. I open door to *bagno.* Ara still sit in corner. She no look at Gogu. I have to do all. I grab Gogu with his legs. I pull him out and to open door. Not far. Alexandru strong. I look at corridor. A man is coming. *Cafone!* Bad time. Door is in middle of him and me. Lucky glass only top part and he no see Gogu on floor. He give me funny look.

I wave to him. He give me ugly *fesso* but keep coming. This bad. I go to door and hold closed. He with other side. I try to make sure he only see me and not Gogu. He try door but I strong.

'I need toilet,' he say.

'Shit,' I say and give him look with the death eyes. 'Bad *puzzo. Molto* shit.' I know he know I lie. But he no want to fight me. I am small but will make him smaller with my fists. 'Go to other.'

He look past or try but I stand in his way. He let go of door and wave as he don't care. But I know he is thinking many things. I see his back only and he go.

I go to Gogu. I lift his back and he sit up like in bed in Our Park of older days. Gone always. I push. He go across floor with legs outside door that is open. I lift Gogu. I push him out door. He fall and go up off ground like a ball. And then go over and over and over many times

very quick and down into grass. This is good. I watch out door to see
only his shoe from grass. I think no one see him here. I go in and shut
door. Gogu rest now.

19

We pretend with the forget. We sleep. Some time gone by. We stop for time in Napoli. Many go off and some more go on. Many Italiano off, some tourist on. We stay on train and now easy for seat. It is good to have seat. Ara not look at me. Not talk to me. She no say yes to me who do this all for her. I want to kiss her. Also to shake. Maybe slap but not good on train. A new person come in and put suitcase up. This man of suit. Then something I not think of. Conductor come back now. I see him in glass. Too late. Can not move. I put my hand on Ara hand and push hard. Hold very hard. But look out of window like I no care.

He open door. Man of suit show conductor ticket. Conductor take and click. I pretend not to see.

'Ticket,' he say.

I pretend not to hear.

'Ticket,'he say again.

'What you say?' I say. 'I show before.'

He look at me. He think many things. 'Where is your ticket?'

'*Si*. I did this. I already show you! It is pack away.'

'I don't remember your face.'

'I did show you, I said.'

'Ticket. *Ora*.'

'I show you but maybe you no like Romanian.'

'Hey. You don't talk to me like that, you little scruff.'

Ara say, 'He is sorry, sir. Please forgive him. His father is very sick. We are going to see him now. Maybe you don't remember him, but I was the one who gave you the ticket. Remember?' Ara give best smile of the kind that is gentle.

The conductor think. 'I think so. *Si.* You are a nice girl. Make sure he is no trouble.'

'No sir. We be very good sir. *Grazie mille.*'

'Well, good luck with your trip.' The conductor leave quick. He no want the trouble, I don't think. *Non lo so.* Maybe he believe her. She has the smile to make believe.

The man of suit look at us. But I give him death eyes. He look away. I look at Ara and smile. But she no look at me.

20

This train. Stop. Where we are is no belong to Aru and Alexandru. It is Pompeii. Many peoples going off quick.

'I know this place,' I say. 'This is very old place like Colosseo. But this have, how do you say…the angry ground that make hot.'

'Volcano?'

'*Si*, this! Let us look.' I stand.

'No. I want nothing!' She still sit.

'This is good place, no? You want to see?'

The man of suit look from the news. I know he no like. I no care.

'Stop this look at me. Look at the paper!'

His eyes go to paper.

Ara look at me. 'We don't have much money. We are not going to spend getting inside tourist place.'

Good for money here more than others.

'We go over fence. No problems.'

'We are supposed to see your sick father. Remember?'

I look back at man in suit with paper. He no look but he is with ears. Maybe later he talk to *carabinieri*.

'Okay. *Si*. You are right. I no wish to be sad. But we still go to Sorrento.' I no like this girl who is right. Or all girls too. All peoples sometimes I no like. Even with pretty *fesso* of Syrian girl. Ara. *Principessa*.

<h1 style="text-align:center">21</h1>

We get off train at Sorrento. All peoples get off. The train no go from here. Only back. Here is mountain. I no see mountain for long time. Many tourists go onto bus at *stazione*. *Molto* little than Roma Termini. Very little.

'Maybe we still go with tourists,' I say. 'They good to hide in life before.'

Ara walk in street with fast legs. She no look at me. I think she okay with me but she is still with angry. I only stand and watch her. This silly girl. Still with beautiful. Still with wish for her body to mine. She walk in little street. To the nice street next. This nice place. Sorrento. Clean. Much little than Roma. Some tourists walk in street too. But many go in bus. They know some place that is better I think. I think if there is tourist then good place to hide. Is also good place to get the money. And good to have Ara to do the singing.

Ara have gone too fast. She get far from me. I run now. The sun is falling for today. We must find place for sleep and better is the food. Too long before the food is in stomach.

I run. I get her. I stop with hold on arm. 'Where you go?' I say. 'You know a place to go?'

'No, I don't.' She pull arm from me.

'Why you go from me?'

Her *fesso* is all red from the crying. 'Why would I want to be with someone who kills? A murderer!'

'Hey. Sshh. Stop with this talking!'

I look for her words. Bad for other people's ears. There is some peoples. They have nice clothes. The places here clean and nice also. I think this Sorrento is only for peoples of *molto* money.

Ara pull back from me. 'I don't know why I am here. I should be with my friends in Roma. They look after me.'

This get me angry. 'You want black man and camel *fesso* better than Alexandru?'

'They are my friends!' She have the tears ready.

'You love Alexandru!'

She shake hard. 'No. You are… I don't want to be with a person who kills.'

I take her arm like to pull donkey. Take to away from peoples. 'I did this not to go to prison. You want to go to prison? I tell you before.'

'No. I don't want to go prison. But you do this without the feeling of the heart. It does not trouble you.' The tears are come.

I look for the ears of other peoples. This not good place for young immigrant.

'What do you say? I do this to protect Ara. To make Ara and Alexandru together. The A names. *Si?*'

She cry much. 'I don't want to be here.'

'*Si.* Be here with Alexandru. You love me.'

She shake her head. 'No. No.'

I take her arms. I want to shake for some time. 'You love me. *Si.* Too many tears now. I am sorry if what I make was bad for you. I no have the parents to say the right and wrong. I have Mama but she go too early. I only be me with the life in the streets. I know this life only. I wish only to be safe. This is not good always. Not real always. This is the life. The life of the streets.'

She shake head. 'No. I have also lived on the streets and the hard life. But not everyone is killing everyone. When does this stop? I want to go back!'

This very hard to take away her words. I slap her. Hard. And tears. 'You be with quiet now. We no go back. We can not. We stay here. We get new life. You sing. We get money. No kill peoples. Okay? We get money. We eat good. Find good place to sleep. Look at sea. Okay? This is good. Now you do what Alexandru say. And do no more.'

She look back with look of the lost *bambini*. She do this before. I like this look. It is better I think. The man is boss. Girl cry too much. Words too much. Not think too much.

I let her go. 'Okay. Good. Now we go find food. *Si*. It is too long for eating for you and me. Okay?'

She turn and walk quick. Away from me. Again. This time, I no have the angry. I gave it all to Ara in the slap. I think the slap good. But it no work. I no follow girl. Alexandru is tired now. I can do no more. Tired with the crying. And the no words. And this hiding in the corner. I let her go.

'Okay. You go! You go but soon you wish to never leave Alexandru. Alexandru the Defender of Mankind! You will wish for me but I tired of your crying and *stupido* words!'

She keep with the walking.

'*Vaffanculo*! *Mignotta*!' I turn. I go to find cigarettes. I have this euro in pocket. I no need girl. Alexandru only need Alexandru.

22

I have the cigarette. I already smoke too many. I wish to drink now. The mosquitoes come to visit Alexandru. Small and more sharp than ones of Roma. The air is different. But still warm. Easy to breathe, I think. Not too away from sea. Sometime on train, I see. Then hide again. I get lost little bit. But now I come back to first street not much away from bus. But Ara not here. I think she crying away at this time. Why she not here? She love Alexandru. I know this. I call her name. I look all around. I run to corner. She not here. I call her name. Only Italiano look back. I don't care for them. I see not many peoples here. Not like Roma.

I run in street. Try to be Ara. Where she go if I think in her head. She must hide from me. Is she real for the no want to return? Maybe she is real with the wish to be away from me. Maybe she no like what I do. I tell her I do this. The bad thing to Gogu I do for her. And for me. And to be safe. She no understand.

I call her name more. I get to the next of the streets. I not know this streets. Which way to go? I pick this one with the lights. I think *ristorante* here. Maybe she sing. *Si*. That is it. She sing to get money for us. She no leave me. She love me. I love her. Ara and Alexandru. The A names. We are together like trees in my park. Side to side. Fix in ground. I find her here. I know. All is good.

I reach the shops. I see only tourists. Old ones. More rich I think. *Molto*. I no care. Ara is all I see. I run again. I call her name. I go to this street and this street. I run and call and the clothes is wet of the sweat and I am pain in stomach. Strong is good but I strong no more. Ara is gone. I feel bad. She has my good with her.

I find gap with two cars and I sit here on road edge. I have my *stupido* camera I can not use. My legs and arms is with the shaking and I can not stop. Then I am with tears like *stupido* girl. My *fesso* is wet and I am making noise like *bambini* but I no stop. I can not stop. Ara. My Ara. I have lost her. I know. I have lost her.

23

I sleep on ground. The sun is make my eyes to open. I sleep all night here. This is bad. *Carabinieri* could see me. I lucky. I think Mama angel soul look over me. I have escape Roma. I am free.

I walk around apartment stalls. Not so many in Roma *centro* but here many. There is no peoples. I think it is weekend day. Maybe Sunday. Too early for tourists. I see lots of clothes. Hang in lots of place. Much space. Make easy to run. I think Alexandru have new clothes now. I find quiet place which is best to take. For Alexandru, this is easy. Like making the piss.

I am back to where I see Ara at the last. I wait. Maybe she come back. I have new clothes. I am better today. I think very tired before. Is better now. I think maybe Syrian girl is no good for me. I no think this A name is good. Must be different no? Too same is no good I think. A and B is better. Ara is too much hiding in this corner. Alexandru no have girl who hiding. Must be strong. Strong like Defender of Mankind. I find Italiano girl. She maybe help me with place to sleep. And food too. Maybe help to get money. Maybe I could get job. No good on streets for too long. Alexandru can do better things than the life of streets.

Maybe I no wait here no more. Maybe I go quick. Go to bus. Follow tourist again. Get away from this Sorrento! Only good for rich peoples. Is not far. I walk to bus which is at train *stazione*. I think I must be quick. If *carabinieri* find Gogu they maybe come here too. But I think not soon. I think Gogu happy in the grass now.

24

I am on bus now. All of tourists and some Italiano. No peoples look at me. With this mirror eyes. They think me tourist too. With my nice clothes. And this camera. I talk to this *Inglese* tourist. Young man. He help me get ticket. Yes I buy ticket! I am real. Like all peoples here. But I am better. But better to pretend to be same like them. I like this pretend game. It is good. I think Alexandru day come again.

This road is little. Like man with no fat. I smell sea. We up high. Go to side of this mountain. There! The sea! It is there! It is real. It is big and flat like big desert. But with the blue, not brown. It look very good. *Tutto buona.*

'Hey, that's some sight, huh?' This white man, tourist, is sit with me.

'*Si.* Is nice.'

Some peoples make photos of the window and the sea outside. And down long way.

'So where you off to then, Jack?' he say.

'Ah. I no understand this Jack.'

He laugh. 'I mean, where are you staying on the coast? *Positano? Amalfi?'*

'*Si.*' The *Inglese* is strange.

He laugh again. He think he better than Alexandru. But I no tell him he lucky. Lucky to not his *fesso* crash against the window.

He say, 'I'm going to Priano. Little fishing village. Very nice by the looks of it. But smaller.' He whisper but I no know why. 'Not so many tourists.'

'*Si.* Me too.'

'Really? You're kidding. Priano?'

'*Si.*' I think follow him is good.

'Oh, cool. Maybe we can work it out together where to get off this thing. You don't know any Italian by any chance, do you?'

'*Si.* Little. Better than *Inglese.*'

'Great! Can you ask the bus driver to let us know when we get to the cemetery? Apparently that's the place to get off. Our stop.'

I ask him explain this word. 'Sematery.' Then when I understand I say, 'It's okay. I do this.'

'Hey, great. We can hang out together one night. Meet up for a few beers. What do you say?'

'Beer. *Si.* I like beer.'

He laugh. I like this laugh. It is laugh born of belly of happy man. I want this laugh too.

I look at big sea. It is good. I smile big. Now I am tourist too.